DOCTOR WHO AND THE CREATURE FROM THE PIT

DOCTOR WHO AND THE CREATURE FROM THE PIT

Based on the BBC television serial by David Fisher by arrangement with the British Broadcasting Corporation

DAVID FISHER

A TARGET BOOK
published by
the paperback division of
W. H. ALLEN & Co. Ltd

A Target Book
Published in 1981
By the Paperback Division of W. H. Allen & Co. Ltd
A Howard & Wyndham Company
44 Hill Street, London W1X 8LB

Made and printed in Great Britain by
The Anchor Press Ltd., Tiptree, Essex

ISBN 0 426 20123 X

Contents

1

The Pit

It was a beautiful day, thought the Lady Adrasta. Hot and humid, of course—which was hardly surprising, since the whole planet was covered with a thick impenetrable jungle—but nonetheless, a beautiful day for an execution.

'No! No! Please ... my lady ... please ...'

The Lady Adrasta ignored the man's cries as her guards dragged him to the edge of the old mineshaft they called the Pit. The wretched engineer had failed her. Those who failed her died. It was a simple rule designed to encourage efficiency amongst her subjects. Some it did; some it didn't. Those it didn't were obviously deliberately refractory and she was better off without them.

The man had become silent, staring in horror down into the darkness below him.

Bored, the Lady Adrasta looked around. The green oppressive jungle seemed almost visibly to be encroaching on the mineshaft. It was encroaching everywhere on the planet, she thought, like a vast green sea.

'Well, what are we waiting for?' she snapped irritably at her Vizier, Madam Karela. 'We haven't got all day.'

The wizened old woman with evil eyes fingered the knife she wore at her waist. All this business of the Pit, she thought, is a waste of time. Why the Pit? Simpler to cut their throats—quicker, too. Still if my lady wanted to indulge her whim …

Karela signalled to the guard who carried the great hunting horn. It was made out of the antler of some huge beast. The guard raised the horn to his lips and blew a single blast, which echoed and re-echoed in the green clearing.

There was a moment of silence, of expectancy. Even the victim fell silent. Everyone waited. Then it came: an answering call from the Pit, inhuman—not animal, either—the sound of some great … what? The victim staring down caught a glimpse of something enormous yet shapeless, moving in the darkness below, and screamed.

The Lady Adrasta nodded to the guards. Two of them seized the poor engineer and hurled him over the edge of the Pit. She watched with interest as he fell amongst the pile of bones, remnants of previous engineers and scientists who had failed her. Then something, a shape, unimaginably huge, and of an extraordinary luminescent green, rolled towards him, covering him.

The man screamed and was silent.

The Lady Adrasta shivered and turned away.

Madam Karela glanced at her mistress and shrugged. The knife, she thought, would be easier, simpler: all this fuss about using the Creature of the Pit.

2

Wolfweeds

Number Four Hold was proving to be a problem. Not surprisingly, reflected Romana. It probably hadn't been cleared out since the day the Doctor had first taken off in the TARDIS from Gallifrey.

She was in the throes of spring-cleaning—an impossible task, as she readily admitted to herself. The TARDIS itself was a multi-dimensional vehicle, which meant that parts of it tended to exist in various times and in different dimensions. You might clear out a cupboard now and five minutes later find it full of the most outlandish objects which had appeared from you had no idea where (or when): like this cardboard box, labelled 'Toys from Hamleys'.

Romana opened the lid and inspected the contents. What on earth had persuaded the Doctor to preserve this collection of useless junk? A single patent-leather dancing pump, signed on the sole 'Love from Fred'; the jawbone of some animal; something that looked like a musical instrument and probably wasn't; a ball of string; a blonde chest-wig. Then suddenly her eye lighted on a familiar sign—the Seal of Gallifrey stamped on an unopened package. Beside the Seal were the words 'INSTAL IMMEDIATELY' and a date. Whatever it was was supposed to have been installed twelve years ago. She unwrapped the package.

The Doctor was enjoying the luxury of being read to. He had programmed K9 with the works of Beatrix Potter and was sitting back listening to the Tale of Peter Rabbit. He looked up irritably when, at a crucial point in the story, Romana entered carrying a piece of equipment.

'What's this?' she asked. 'I found it in Number Four Hold.'

'Oh, some useless piece of junk. Chuck it away.'

K9, ever helpful, knew better.

'It's a Mark 3 Emergency Transceiver, mistress,' he explained.

'What's it for?' asked Romana.

'To receive and send distress calls, mistress.'

But the Doctor wasn't impressed. The authorities on Gallifrey were always sending him new pieces of equipment to try out. If he wasted his valuable time installing every new gimmick they sent him, he would never have time for the really important things.

'Like listening to the Tale of Peter Rabbit?' suggested Romana.

The Doctor decided to overlook that remark. 'In any case,' he declared, marshalling what he regarded as the ultimate argument, 'what was the point of installing a Distress Transceiver when I was never in distress.' Seeing Romana's reaction, he added hastily, 'Well, not often. Not what you'd call often.'

'The Transceiver plugs into the central console, mistress,' observed K9.

'Thank you, K9,' replied Romana plugging in the equipment and switching on.

Immediately the TARDIS was filled with a wild screeching noise, a high-pitched babble of sound as if something were screaming hysterically.

The Doctor and Romana put their hands over their ears, but only for a moment, because suddenly the TARDIS tilted at a mad angle and both of them were hurled into a heap in the corner. A moment or two later the TARDIS righted itself. It had landed somewhere. The Doctor staggered to his feet and switched off the Transceiver. He turned to Romana. 'Now you know why I never installed that thing,' he observed. 'It never worked properly.'

'Correction, master,' said K9. 'That is how it is supposed to work.'

But the Doctor had switched on the scanning screen and was too busy studying their landing place to reply. 'Good Lord,' he exclaimed. 'Incredible.'

From her position on the floor Romana looked up at the screen. All she could see was jungle: green, impenetrable jungle, and something huge and curved that rose into the air.

When Romana joined the Doctor outside, she found him studying this enormous structure with interest. Because of the jungle, it was difficult to make out its size, let alone its purpose. But seemed to be about 400 metres long and it rose unevenly to a height of about 10 metres. The top was serrated as if broken by some force. Surely it couldn't be a wall—it was only a few centimetres thick.

'What is it?' she asked.

'An egg, of course,' replied the Doctor. 'Or at least part of the shell. Have a look round and see if you can find the rest of it.'

Romana stared at the thing in astonishment. It scarcely seemed possible. And yet now she came to look at the structure there was something egg-like about it. But what kind of creature could have laid an egg 400 metres long?

'I'll tell you something else,' went on the Doctor, scratching at the shell with his penknife. 'This thing's made of metal. Did you say something?' he enquired politely.

'No,' replied Romana. 'I think what you heard was just my mind boggling. Metal birds laying metal eggs. Though I suppose it doesn't have to be a bird, does it? Other things lay eggs.'

The Doctor had taken an electronic stethoscope from his pocket and had placed the receiver against the shell. 'It's alive,' he announced. 'The shell. Listen.'

Romana took the stethoscope. She heard a high-pitched babble of sound. It was the same sound they had heard in the TARDIS over the Emergency Transceiver. 'Whoever heard of an eggshell sending a distress call?' she demanded. 'There has to be a transmitter somewhere. It stands to reason.'

The Doctor was intrigued by the phrase. Why should you stand to reason. It didn't make sense. Why didn't you lie down to reason? So much more sensible: rests the cerebellum. He was just about to remark on the fact when he realised that Romana had gone—searching for the transmitter no doubt. Still, why shouldn't an eggshell transmit a distress call—particularly if it was broken?

A rustling sound in the jungle momentarily disturbed him. He looked round. No sign of anyone. The jungle was still, except for a round green puff-ball like a tumbleweed. Its fronds were waving gently as if disturbed by a breeze. The Doctor returned to his examination of the shell. There was no doubt it was made of the most extraordinary material. It looked as if it had been woven.

Again there was a rustling sound. The Doctor turned round. Curious: there were now three tumbleweeds, or whatever they were, in the clearing behind him. A second later, when he looked round again, there were four tumbleweeds behind him. Suddenly, as he looked, one of the weeds floated across the clearing and attached itself to the sleeve of his coat. They were big things, the size of a barrel. When he tried to pull the thing off him, he found that he couldn't. The weed was covered with curious hooked thorns, like claws. Another weed floated across the clearing and attached itself to his leg. When a third attached itself to him, he discovered he was helpless. 'Romana! Romana!' he called. But she didn't hear him. She had walked round to the far side of the shell and was trying to get some idea of the actual size of the thing.

The weight of the weeds dragged him to the ground. More were already emerging from the jungle into the clearing. In a moment they took flight too and attached themselves to him. Desperately he tried to drag himself away round the curve of the egg. In doing so, he ran into a boot. The Doctor clutched it thankfully and looked into the face of its owner, the sight of whom was not comforting. A grim-faced, leather-clad individual looked down at him. In his hand he held a long sword with a serrated blade.

'Could you get these things off me?' asked the Doctor. 'Please.'

A whip cracked. It was wielded by another leather-clad figure who emerged from the jungle. The weeds seemed to cringe. They immediately released the Doctor and, like obedient hounds, took their position behind the huntsman.

'Thank you,' said the Doctor attempting to rise. But the first man put his foot on his chest and looked to the huntsman for orders.

'Kill him,' ordered the huntsman.

The other man swung his long sword and prepared to split open the Doctor's skull.

'I don't want to stand on protocol,' observed the Doctor, 'but shouldn't you at least take me to your leader before you do anything we'd both be sorry for later.'

The man looked at the huntsman for instructions. He in turn looked at the wizened old woman all in black, who had just appeared round the side of the eggshell. She drove Romana before her at knife point.

'Leave him,' said Madam Karela. 'We'll kill him later.'

'Thank you,' replied the Doctor gratefully. He rose to his feet and dusted himself down. The weeds rustled angrily behind the huntsman, who cracked his whip.

'What are those things?'

'Wolfweeds,' declared Madam Karela.

'Weeds? Plants?'

'Specially grown in the Lady Adrasta's nurseries,' explained Madam Karela. 'We use them for hunting.'

'Hunting what?'

'Criminals.'

The Doctor regarded the botanical hounds with some trepidation. 'Have you tried getting her interested in geraniums instead?' he enquired. 'Much safer. And they bloom, too.'

But Madam Karela ignored such pleasantries.

'What are you doing in the Place of Death?' she asked.

'Why do you call it that?' asked the Doctor.

'Because anyone found here is automatically put to death.'

'I trust you make exceptions,' remarked the Doctor.

But from the look of Madam Karela, he realised that she never made exceptions. However, she was interested in the TARDIS. 'It travels?' she enquired. 'How? It's got no wheels.'

The Doctor offered to show her, but just at that moment the Wolfweeds began to rustle and their thorns started making a curious clacking noise. The huntsman declared that they sensed danger. Bandits were approaching. Madam Karela ordered everyone to be ready to move out.

The soldiers locked the Doctor into what looked like portable stocks. His head and hands were held in a kind of wooden yoke, leaving him free to walk. Madam Karela climbed into her litter. With soldiers and Wolfweeds guarding her, the procession left the Place of Death and plunged into the jungle. The Doctor and Romana, surrounded by guards, brought up the rear.

The attack, when it came, was swift and decisive. A horde of stocky, lank-haired men, wearing skins and wielding clubs, suddenly appeared out of nowhere. It was all over in a matter of seconds. Leaving two soldiers and one of their own number dead, the men vanished into the jungle again.

It was a minute or two before the Doctor realised that Romana had gone. She had been abducted by the wild men.

3

The Doctor's Leap to Death

'Here she is,' said the small, pockmarked bandit, thrusting her into the cave.

Romana looked around. Her captors were a rough-looking lot, dressed in filthy skins and rags. Their living conditions were obviously no more attractive than their personal appearance. The cave was small, damp, and smelt of wood smoke and rancid cooking fat. Crouched by a fire that burned smokily in the darkness, was a tattered figure crooning to himself, as he drooled over a small collection of metal junk, which was piled up on an animal skin. The collection contained nothing of any value as far as Romana could see: old nails, bits of broken cooking vessels, tools—all lovingly polished. Torvin hastily covered the bandits' haul of metal and regarded Romana suspiciously. 'What's that?' he demanded.

'One of Adrasta's ladies-in-waiting,' replied Edu, the pockmarked one. 'I think.'

Romana decided not to disabuse him of this notion. Being a lady-in-waiting indicated at least a certain social position on the planet. However, Torvin's reply was not reassuring.

'Kill her,' he said.

'But we could ransom her,' objected Edu. 'She might be valuable.'

'How many times do I have to tell you, prisoners are only valuable if they're made of metal,' pointed out Torvin. 'Has she got metal legs?'

Edu regarded Romana's full-length skirt with interest.

'No,' said Romana.

Torvin shrugged and drew his finger across his throat.

'Is he your leader?' Romana enquired.

'No,' replied Edu. 'He's Torvin.'

'I'm the brains of this gang,' declared Torvin. 'The planner. I plan, they go out and do what I planned. It works very well. Look at that.' He pointed proudly to the hoard of metal. 'Bet you've never seen as much metal as that all together at one time, have you? Get on with it,' he said to Edu, who drew a rusty knife from his belt and felt the blade with his thumb.

'If he's not your leader, why do you always do what he says?' enquired Romana.

'I don't,' replied Edu. 'We all have a vote.'

'But nobody voted,' objected Romana.

Edu, Ainu and the other bandits turned on Torvin.

'So vote,' replied the latter. 'Vote ... then kill her.'

The Castle rose out of the jungle like a great black sea-beast rising from the green depths. The thick outer walls kept the jungle at bay—though for how much longer, wondered the Doctor. Already leaves and creepers were growing up the walls, forcing their hair-like roots into the mortar, cracking even the great stone blocks themselves.

The procession wound through the imposing gateway. When the last of the Wolfweeds had entered the courtyard, the massive doors swung to behind them, shutting out the oppressive jungle.

The huntsman shouted and cracked his whip, driving the Wolfweeds off to their kennels. Or was it hothouses, in view of the fact that they were plants? The Doctor wondered what Lady Adrasta fed them on: dried blood?

Still wearing his yoke, the Doctor followed Madam Karela up the steps into the outer hall of the Castle. Beyond lay the audience chambers of the Lady Adrasta. He was about to follow the black-robed Vizier into the presence of Adrasta, when the old woman gestured to the guards to restrain him.

The Doctor waited. He walked up and down, whistling to himself, watching the guards. There were only two on duty. They were bored. Locked into the yoke he was wearing, the Doctor wasn't going to get away. Or so they thought. But the Doctor had other ideas.

The Doctor tried to scratch his nose. But with his hands locked at shoulder level, about four feet apart, it was obviously an impossibility.

'Could you scratch my nose?' he asked the guards.

The guards, as guards will, conferred. There was nothing in guardroom orders to suggest that they should not assist a prisoner. On the other hand, there was nothing to suggest they should.

'Look,' suggested the Doctor. 'Just put your hand out and I'll rub my nose on it.'

As the guard put his hand to the Doctor's nose, he swung the heavy wooden yoke. One end caught the first guard in the side of the head and the other end smashed against the second guard's jaw. Both men dropped as if poleaxed. The Doctor stepped over their recumbent forms and made for the door.

'Do let me take that thing off,' said a woman's voice. 'It must be frightfully uncomfortable.'

The Doctor turned to find himself face to face with a tall, remarkably handsome woman with dark hair. She ignored the unconscious guards and unlocked the Doctor's hands from the yoke, which she handed to Madam Karela.

'You would be the Lady Adrasta,' observed the Doctor.

'And you would be the fellow who was found at the Place of Death,' she replied.

He wished they wouldn't keep calling it by that name. It made him distinctly uneasy. He followed Adrasta into the audience chamber. He heard the guards groan and out of the corner of his eye saw Madam Karela kicking them savagely.

'What did you make of the Object at the Place of Death?' asked Adrasta. 'You know, some of the finest brains on Chloris have spent years trying to unravel the problem. What did you make of it?'

'It's an egg,' replied the Doctor.

Surprised, Adrasta stopped in her tracks. 'Are you sure? Have you ever seen anything like it before?'

The Doctor had to admit that he hadn't. Nor had he any idea what kind of creature might have laid such a huge thing. However, he was more interested at the moment in rescuing Romana than in a theoretical discussion about the nature of the Object.

'Of course,' agreed Adrasta sympathetically. 'I understand. I'll send a troop of guards immediately. Madam Karela will take personal command of the rescue operations.' The older woman saluted and left the audience chamber. 'Don't worry,' said Adrasta. 'My Wolfweeds will find your companion. Madam Karela is very efficient.'

'What will the bandits do to Romana?' asked the Doctor.

'Kill her quickly—if she's lucky.'

'And if she's not?'

'Then,' said Adrasta with a sympathetic smile, 'they will kill her very, very slowly.'

The democratic process had run its course. Unfortunately only the pockmarked Edu had voted for Romana's continued survival, and he hardly looked cut out for the role of a knight in shining armour. Romana rewarded him with a dazzling smile which brought a blush to his pitted cheeks.

Torvin meanwhile rubbed his hands, delighted at having his original decisions upheld by the gang. 'All right, my lovely boys,' he declared. 'We're all agreed now. Six votes to one. We kill her.'

'Who'll do it?' asked Ainu.

'You can,' replied Torvin generously.

'Suppose the Lady Adrasta finds out,' objected Ainu.

'She won't.'

'But supposing she did?'

Romana detected in the faces of Torvin's gang a certain lack of enthusiasm for the task. Unimpressive they might be, but she had no doubt that they would eventually carry out their threat. It was now time, she decided, to take a more decisive hand in events.

Torvin and his men were arguing amongst themselves as to who would do the deed and how. 'It doesn't matter what you use,' shouted Torvin. 'Knife, club or leetrobe*. Just kill her!'

'Go ahead,' said Romana, more calmly than she felt. 'Kill me. Commit suicide if you must.'

'Don't listen to her,' warned Torvin. 'She's only trying to scare you. Kill her!'

'If you murdered one of her ladies-in-waiting, Adrasta would hunt you down with her guards and her Wolfweeds, wouldn't she?' demanded Romana. 'No matter how long it took, no matter where you went.'

The members of the gang looked uneasy. They seemed in no doubt that that was precisely what Adrasta would do. Whoever this Adrasta was, reflected Romana, she must be pretty formidable; the thought of her obviously terrified this bunch of incompetents.

'So what do you think she would do if you murdered an important visitor to her planet?' Romana continued.

'She's just trying to save her own skin!' screamed Torvin. 'Don't listen to her.'

Ainu, who was hairier, if less pockmarked, than Edu, made a clumsy attempt at a bow. 'Who are you, my lady?' he asked Romana.

Romana smiled. She almost felt like patting the unappetising little man on the top of his filthy head.

'That,' she observed kindly, 'is the first sensible question I have been asked since you brought me here.' She drew herself up to her full height. 'I am an intergalactic traveller and a Time Lady,' she declared proudly. 'And I am not used to being assaulted and held captive by a collection of grubby, hairy little men.'

*A leetrobe is a species of giant flowering lettuce unique to Chloris.

This was too much for Torvin, who could see he was on the verge of losing the argument. He seized his club and came at her. The others grabbed him before he could club her to the ground.

'Sit down!' snapped Romana. 'This minute.' Sheepishly the men squatted on their haunches. 'That's better,' said Romana and took from around her neck the whistle that summoned K9 and put it to her lips. Torvin snatched it away from her.

'What's this?' he demanded.

'It's a whistle,' said Romana. 'Blow through it if you don't believe me.'

Torvin put it to his lips and blew long and hard. But there was no sound they could hear because its whistle operated at higher frequencies than the human ear could register. Nevertheless, inside the TARDIS, which rested by the huge eggshell at the Place of Death, K9 responded. His micro-circuiting was activated by the stimulus of the whistle. 'Coming, mistress,' he said in his high-pitched mechanical voice.

Back in the bandits' cave, Torvin looked at the whistle in disgust. 'It doesn't work,' he complained.

'Keep blowing,' advised Romana. 'Something'll happen soon enough.'

'You said you had some theories about this eggshell,' enquired the Lady Adrasta.

But the Doctor was staring in fascination at something that hung on the wall of the audience chamber. It looked like a huge circular shield, with a great boss in the centre. But it obviously wasn't a shield because when he touched it, the material it was made of felt almost like living flesh.

'Did you hear me, Doctor?' demanded the Lady Adrasta.

'Yes, yes. Where did this thing come from?'

'It was found in the jungle about fifteen years ago,' replied Adrasta. 'Tell me about the shell. My huntsman heard you say it was alive.'

'Alive? It's screaming in pain,' said the Doctor. He touched the shield again. 'What is it, do you know?'

'No!' declared Adrasta and returned to the subject that interested her. 'If the shell is screaming as you say, why can no one hear it?'

'Because it's only detectable at very low frequencies. That's why.' He took out his penknife and tried to scratch the shield. But his knife made no impression: flesh-like yet impervious to a sharp instrument—extra-ordinary.

'What is the shell screaming about?' demanded Adrasta.

'More to the point,' replied the Doctor, 'for whom is it screaming? It's mother? If so, the mind boggles. Just think of the size of Mummy.'

But the Lady Adrasta had heard enough. She crossed the room and drew back a hanging which covered a low doorway. In the doorway stood two men in long black robes, looking like a pair of unemployed undertakers. Adrasta introduced them as two of her engineers, Doran and Tollund.

'You heard?' she asked the engineers.

'Perfectly,' replied Tollund, the older and more senior of the two.

'He is quite wrong,' declared Doran. 'In my latest paper on the subject I prove conclusively, on astrological and astronomical grounds, that the structure that stands in the Place of Death, that he calls an egg, is in fact the remains of an ancient temple.'

'Rubbish,' said the Doctor. 'It's an egg.'

Tollund shook his head. 'Have you considered the implications?' he asked. 'A bird large enough to lay an egg that size would have a wingspan of at least a mile.'

But the Doctor was not to be dissuaded. 'It isn't only birds who lay eggs,' he pointed out. 'Fish do, too.'

'On land?' scoffed Doran. He turned to Adrasta. 'My lady ...'

'Reptiles lay eggs,' said the Doctor.

'My lady, this man is being ...'

'So do frogs.'

'... frivolous.'

'He's right, you know,' confessed the Doctor. 'It's a fatal flaw in my character.'

Doran shook his head pityingly. It was obvious that this odd visitor knew very little science. But perhaps he would prove amenable to logical argument and the weight of genuine scholarship. 'How do you account for the marks of intense heat on the exterior of the shell?' he asked.

'Perhaps someone tried to fry it,' suggested the Doctor mischieviously.

The man was absurd; a charlatan of some sort, decided Doran. He turned to the Lady Adrasta and shrugged. But if he was looking for sympathy, he found none. Adrasta glared at the unfortunate engineer.

'I saw no mention in your paper that the shell was alive, Engineer Doran,' she said in a voice cold enough to freeze mercury.

'Of course you didn't, my lady. Because it isn't. It

can't be alive.' Desperately he looked to Tollund for support, but his superior avoided his eyes. Bravely Doran ploughed on. 'Our instruments have detected absolutely no sign of life in the shell.'

'His did,' replied Adrasta, indicating the Doctor.

'Perhaps I had an unfair advantage,' remarked the Doctor.

'Better equipment?'

'An open mind.'

But the Lady Adrasta was in no mood for pleasantries. Engineer Doran had failed her. Those who failed her died. It was a simple rule designed to ensure the total dedication of all who served her. She regarded Doran almost with regret. He was a not unattractive young man, and once he had even shown signs of brilliance. There was a time when she had considered replacing Tollund with Doran. It was a pity he had failed to live up to his promise. 'Take him!' she ordered the guards.

Terrified, knowing what his fate would be, Doran sank to his knees. 'My lady, I beg you . . .' But the guards seized him and dragged him away.

Adrasta turned to the Doctor. 'Since you know a lot more about that shell than you seemed prepared to say, perhaps this little demonstration will encourage you to be more co-operative in future.'

Romana was curious. 'Why did you become bandits?' she asked.

'Because the Lady Adrasta closed down the mine,' explained Edu.

'So you're really miners, then?'

The seven bandits nodded their heads forlornly. Romana looked at them. Of course, she thought, that would explain everything. As bandits they were hopeless. They were probably the most ill-organised, unprofessional collection of criminals she had ever met in her travels through umpteen galaxies and only the TARDIS knew how many hundreds of thousands of years.

'Why did Adrasta close the mine?' she asked.

'Because of the Creature,' said Ainu.

'What Creature? Where did it come from?'

The seven little men shook their heads. One day, as usual, they had reported for work at the mine and found the Creature in residence. It was huge and filled every corner of the mine, like some vast earthworm.

'I think it must have lain in the earth for centuries until our mining disturbed it,' declared one of the miners.

The others nodded in agreement.

'So that's why metal became scarce!' exclaimed Romana. 'That's why the jungle started to encroach everywhere. You had no tools to cut it back.'

'There never was very much metal available,' said Edu. 'Adrasta owned the only working mine.'

'I wouldn't say metal was scarce,' declared Torvin laying a grubby protective hand on their hoard. 'For us at any rate. Eh, lads?'

Romana looked at the pathetic pile of junk. 'Is that the best you could do?'

Torvin quivered with indignation. 'That's the result of scores of daring raids,' he said. 'All meticulously planned, all timed to the second. We've risked our lives a dozen times over for this little lot.'

'*We* have, you mean,' objected Ainu. 'I don't recall

you risking anything. You just stay here and keep the booty well polished, while we go out and face Adrasta's guards and Wolfweeds.'

Torvin waved his objection aside. 'Someone has to plan. Someone has to organise. Someone has to be the brains behind our success.'

'You call this success?' scoffed Romana. 'I must be quite frank with you, gentlemen: as bandits you're hardly in the Jesse James class.'

The bandits stared at her blankly. Romana decided she didn't have time to educate Torvin and his band in the details of Western mythology. It was time for her to go. She could hear the approaching whirr of K9. She rose to her feet.

'Well, I must be going now.'

'You're going nowhere,' declared Torvin. He turned to the others. 'I've been thinking. Perhaps you were right. Perhaps we can ransom her. Maybe Adrasta will pay a sack or two of metal for our lady traveller.'

'I should think it most unlikely,' said Romana. 'Anyway I'm afraid you'll never find out.'

At that moment K9 entered the cave. The bandits stared at the apparition in astonishment. They had never seen a mechanical animal before. Torvin was the first to appreciate the value of K9. He positively drooled at the thought.

'It's made of metal! All made of real metal! It must be worth a fortune.'

Picking up his club, he approached K9, who swivelled to meet him, keeping his sensors and ray gun trained on the bandit.

'Goodbye, gentlemen,' said Romana. 'I can't honestly say it's been a pleasure.'

Torvin waved her to go. 'Go if you want to. But you're leaving that thing here. Think what he's worth, lads!' he said to the others. 'All that metal.'

'K9,' ordered Romana.

Switching his ray gun to stun, K9 stopped Torvin in his tracks.

'It's all right, he's not dead,' explained Romana kindly. 'He'll come to in a minute—with a very sore head. But then I expect you're used to that.'

With K9 covering her retreat she left the cave.

It was a typical mineshaft—with a windlass and rope descending into the depths. But the sight of it seemed to terrify Doran the engineer, who was held between the two guards. At a signal from Adrasta one of the guards blew a single blast on a large horn.

'What is this place?' asked the Doctor, staring fascinated down the shaft.

'We call it the Pit.'

The echoes of the horn call died and there was a moment of silence, a moment of expectancy. Then from the bowels of the earth, from the very depths of the Pit, came an answering call, inhuman, yet not animal either—the sound of some great ... thing.

The guards put ropes round Doran's shoulders, attached them to the windlass, then pushed the terrified man so that he swung over the Pit. The engineer screamed and begged for his life.

The Doctor intervened. 'Look,' he said to Adrasta. 'I don't know what you're planning, but I suggest you think again. Engineer Doran may be a bit of an idiot, but at least he's a reasonably conscientious idiot. And even bad engineers are hard to come by this side of the galaxy.'

But Adrasta wasn't listening. She was staring downwards into the Pit, waiting for something. Her expression was almost lustful, as if she were awaiting for a lover to appear.

Once again the guard blew upon the horn. And once again from the depths of the Pit, though nearer this time, came the answering call.

'What is it?' asked the Doctor.

At a sign from Adrasta the guards began to lower the screaming engineer down into the Pit.

The call came again, closer still: neither human nor animal, the sound of some great ... thing ... baying—whether in anger or agony or merely hunger, the Doctor could not tell. He joined Adrasta on the platform at the edge of the Pit and stared down into the depths.

They saw Doran reach the bottom. At a sign from Adrasta the guards cut the windlass rope. Down below they watched Doran free himself. The man looked around in obvious terror.

The thing—whatever it was—was coming closer. The Doctor could smell it: a strange metallic odour, like silver polish or a run-down battery. He stared into the darkness below wondering what was about to appear. A rush of foul, fetid air surged up the mineshaft. The Creature must be enormous, he realised. It was acting like a giant piston, filling the shafts and corridors of the mine, driving the exhausted air upwards.

Then suddenly something vast and shapeless, something that was a livid purulent green, covered the bottom of the Pit. Doran screamed once, and then his cries were cut short as the immensity of the Creature flowed inexorably over him.

Adrasta turned to the Doctor. 'That is what happens to those who fail me.'

Unseen by the guards, undetected by the Wolfweeds, K9 and Romana emerged from the jungle. Everyone was stood around the mineshaft staring into the depths.

'K9,' whispered Romana, 'fire at the first sign of trouble.'

'Understood, mistress.'

'Doctor!' she called.

The Doctor and Adrasta reacted instantly.

'Seize her!' snarled Adrasta to her guards.

'Run for it!' shouted the Doctor. 'Quick. It's your only chance.'

The guards immediately converged on Romana.

'Stand back!' she cried. 'I'm warning you. I have K9.'

K9 turned his nose laser onto the first guard and stopped him in his tracks. Another guard went down a moment later. Adrasta shouted for the Wolfweeds. The huntsman cracked his whip and the strange plants drifted over to K9. The first was incinerated by the robot. It made a curious mewing sound, like a lost kitten, and burst into flames. A second Wolfweed was turned into charcoal. A third was badly singed. But by now the others had reached K9. They fastened themselves to his sensors, to his metal sides, to his back. In a moment he was submerged beneath half a dozen of the plants.

'K9!' cried Romana in alarm. There was silence, no movement from within the mass of plants. 'K9!'

The Doctor meanwhile had been investigating the Pit. The Creature seemed to have withdrawn. The end of the windlass rope still hung part of the way down the mineshaft.

When the huntsman cracked his whip and drove the Wolfweeds away from the robot, Romana saw that K9 was motionless. He was covered in an impenetrable cocoon of fibres or hair. The Wolfweeds had wrapped him in something resembling a spider's web.

'Don't worry, my dear,' said Adrasta. 'The little creature is only paralysed.' She turned to the Doctor triumphantly. 'Well, Doctor,' she said, 'I have your companion, your mechanical animal and you. It seems that I hold all the cards now.'

'Not quite,' replied the Doctor. And he seized the windlass rope and leapt into the Pit.

4

The Creature

Horrified, Romana saw the Doctor plunge into the Pit. Ignoring everyone, she ran to the edge, hoping that somehow he had managed to cling to the walls of the old mineshaft.

'Seize her!' cried Adrasta.

Two of the guards converged upon Romana.

'Let me go down to him,' she pleaded, struggling in their arms. 'He may be hurt.'

Adrasta waved her aside. 'He's dead by now,' she replied. 'No one can save him from the Creature, certainly not you. You're too valuable to lose.'

Romana stared blankly at the woman. 'Valuable? What do you mean?'

'Because now he's gone, you're the only one left who knows anything about that huge broken shell at the Place of Death.' Adrasta stared down into the Pit, a look of regret on her face. 'He discovered something about it that none of my scientists had even guessed in fifteen years. What a waste! He just did it to guarantee your survival.'

'My survival?'

Adrasta regarded Romana with cold pitiless eyes. 'While he was alive, I had no need of you. You were dispensable. But now you're heir to all the Doctor's secrets. At least,' she added with a smile that sent a shiver down

Romana's spine, 'I hope you are. Anyway we'll soon find out.'

The guards lashed the immobile K9 between two stout branches, and four of them lifted the robot and took him away. Everything of metal was of value on this god-forsaken planet, thought Romana, otherwise K9 would have joined the Doctor at the bottom of the Pit. She started suddenly as the Lady Adrasta put an arm around her.

'Come along, my dear,' said the Lady. 'We've a lot to talk about.' She looked towards the mineshaft and her expression softened. 'Believe me,' she added, 'he's dead. No one comes out of the Pit alive.'

This was a conclusion the Doctor was beginning to share.

He was clinging to an outcrop of rock halfway down the mineshaft. He had noticed it when he had looked into the Pit. Funny how it seemed to have shrunk. From above it had appeared to be a sizeable ledge, big enough to sit on. Now he was down here it seemed little more than a fingerhold—and not a very secure one at that. With his free hand he tried to drive a piton—fortunately he had several in his pockets, along with a hammer—into the rock face, and discovered that it was anything but simple. The rock face seemed as hard as... well... rock. The trouble was it all looked so easy in the books. He kept trying to remember what that charming little Nepalese fellow had told him. What was his name now? Tensing, was it? The Doctor gave a last despairing bang at the piton and then tested it very gingerly to see if it would bear his weight. Ah, it would. Excellent. Now for the next piton.

The second piton went in more easily than the first. A

third was driven in, and the Doctor began to feel that there was nothing to this mountaineering lark after all. It was just a matter of employing very basic principles of mechanics—the kind of thing old Isaac Newton had been so good at formulating.

When it came to the fourth piton, the Doctor discovered that he had left the hammer behind on the ledge. Passing his scarf through the third piton, the Doctor hung on and leaned back to reach for the hammer. Unused to such treatment his scarf suddenly stretched. It stretched again. The third piton loosened.

For a moment the Doctor hung there in space by his scarf, turning slowly like a chicken on a spit, watching the third piton gently ease itself out of the rock face. Then with a muffled yell the Doctor fell.

'I should have paid more attention to that little Tensing fellow,' was his last thought before he landed in a heap on something soft and wet. It turned out to be Engineer Doran. Something has crushed him to a pulp.

'Sorry, old boy,' said the Doctor, rising to his feet. Then he realised the engineer was unable to acknowledge his apology.

From the shaft the Pit broadened out into a large cavern from which radiated several tunnels. The Doctor inspected each tunnel. Six ways presented themselves: which one to take? Blackness and fetid air greeted him at each opening. Then faintly, but growing louder all the time, he heard an extraordinary sound, not human, not animal; a sudden rush of air down one of the tunnels; a smell of old batteries. The Doctor backed away. The Creature, whatever it was, was coming closer.

'What is that thing in the Pit?' asked Romana. She was

in the Lady Adrasta's audience chamber, facing the formidable ruler of Chloris herself.

'We call it the Creature,' replied the Lady Adrasta.

That's original, thought Romana. But what kind of Creature is it?

As if replying to her unasked question, Adrasta explained that the thing had no shape. It was vast. It was an amorphous mass that oozed through the tunnels like jelly. 'Our researchers,' went on Adrasta, 'divide into two categories: those who have been close enough to find out something about the Creature and ...'

'And?' prompted Romana.

'And those who are still alive.'

'All the same,' insisted Romana, 'you must know something about the beast.'

'It kills people,' replied Adrasta. 'What more is there to know?'

Romana could think of quite a few things, but the Lady Adrasta was obviously not disposed to discuss the Creature. It just didn't make sense. Here was a real live monster oozing like toothpaste around the tunnels of what appeared to be the only mine on the planet, gobbling up failed engineers like so many cocktail canapes, and preventing the mine from being worked. And if any planet desperately needed metal it was Chloris. You could almost see the jungle encroaching as you watched.

'Tell me about the shell you found at the Place of Death.'

What in the name of the Mudmen of Epsilon Eridani did the rotten old shell matter? The Doctor had claimed it was the remains of an egg, but Romana wasn't convinced it was.

'Why are you so interested in the shell?' she demanded.

The Lady Adrasta looked up from admiring herself in an ornate hand mirror. 'There are some questions,' she said, 'it is wiser not to ask. Now tell me about the shell.'

'There are some questions,' replied Romana, 'it is wiser not to—' Without any perceptible change of expression Adrasta leaned forward and struck her savagely across the face. Romana staggered back, her head ringing from the blow.

'Now, my dear,' said Adrasta sweetly, 'I'll ask you just once more: are you going to tell me what you know about the shell?'

Romana rubbed her cheek and stared into the cold eyes of the ruler of Chloris. She was aware that she had come very close to death. 'I'll tell you whatever you want to know,' she said.

The Lady Adrasta nodded. 'Good. I was sure you would, my dear. I just know we'll get along famously. Now ...'

Fortunately before she could question Romana further, some of the guards entered carrying the immobile K9. They put the robot on a table.

'What are you going to do with him?' asked Romana.

'Break him up, of course,' explained Adrasta. 'On this planet metal is far too valuable to waste on mere toys.'

Romana's heart sank as she stared at K9 trapped in the web the Wolfweeds had spun around him. He looked like some strange chrysalis immured in a cocoon. An idea began to germinate. If his power packs had not been damaged, perhaps she could yet show this monstrous woman that K9 was anything but a toy.

Round a bend in the tunnel the Doctor caught a glimpse of something huge. It filled the tunnel from floor to roof. It was a livid putrescent green. It flowed towards him like a solid wall of slime.

The Doctor turned and fled. He found a narrower tunnel, half-filled with rocks which had fallen when there had been a cave-in. Scrambling desperately over the obstruction he tried to put as much distance as possible between himself and the Creature. The mine was honeycombed with passages, some large enough to drive a truck through, some no more than narrow crawls big enough to take one miner at a time. The prospect of being caught in one of those with the Creature oozing remorselessly towards him made the Doctor shiver.

The trouble with the sight of a moving wall of slime, he reflected, was that it drove every thought of scientific investigation from one's mind. Next time I won't panic—that is, if I'm unfortunate enough for there to be a next time.

His foot struck something on the floor of the tunnel—something hollow that rolled. The Doctor felt in his pocket for a match, found one, and struck it on the wall of the tunnel. He bent to pick up the hollow thing his foot had struck—and found himself face to face with a human skull. 'Perhaps after all,' he said to the skull, 'one should temper one's enthusiasm for scientific enquiry with a modicum of caution.' The skull seemed to agree.

Suddenly his nostrils were assailed with that extraordinary smell, like old batteries. And he felt, rather than heard, a movement in the darkness. A movement of air as if driven by some giant piston. The tunnel was irradiated with a greenish glow, like the light that shines from putrescent meat.

The Doctor backed cautiously away.

Something slid round the corner of the tunnel. It was like a shapeless hand composed of green slime. With repulsive delicacy it elongated itself, reaching blindly down the tunnel in the direction of the Doctor.

The Doctor backed against the rock face, trying to find a way out, but the tunnel seemed to be a dead end . . .

In the great audience chamber of the Lady Adrasta's Palace an extraordinary scene was in progress.

A guard swung a sledge hammer and brought it crashing down on K9's head, which was still wrapped in the web spun by the Wolfweeds. The guard was a powerful man and it was the third time the hammer had struck K9. Romana couldn't stand anymore. She had no way of knowing how much damage the Wolfweeds had done to the robot.

'Stop him!' she screamed. 'That maniac will damage his circuitry.'

The Lady Adrasta gave no sign. The guard swung the hammer once again.

'Look, I'll do anything you want,' cried Romana. 'Only don't destroy him.'

The Lady Adrasta held up her hand. The guard arrested the blow, but remained poised to strike, awaiting further orders.

'You'll tell me all about your travelling machine?' she asked.

Romana gave in. 'All right. But if that moron doesn't stop trying to hammer K9 into sheet metal, it won't do you any good. Everything you want to know is locked in

K9's memory banks. Damage them and you'll never learn anything.'

'Is that a threat?' demanded the Lady Adrasta.

'It's a fact.'

The Lady Adrasta signalled the guard to lower his hammer. She came over to the bewebbed K9 and stroked him.

'So the little metal animal knows everything.' She turned a smile of dazzling sweetness on Romana. 'That makes both you and the Doctor redundant, doesn't it, my dear?'

'Not quite,' replied Romana, only too aware of what happened to those whom the Lady Adrasta found to be redundant. Out of the corner of her eye she could see Madam Karela sliding the knife from her belt, ready to do her mistress's bidding. 'You see, I'm the only one who can operate K9. Without me he can't tell you what you want to know.'

The Lady Adrasta considered the information for a moment. Very probably the girl was lying. She was after all a stranger to the planet. She had yet to learn that lying to the Lady Adrasta was a dangerous occupation. On the other hand, if what she said was true ... Adrasta signalled to Madam Karela to put her knife away.

A hand gripped the Doctor's shoulder—just as the tentacle from the Creature was about to touch him.

The Doctor turned to find himself face to face with a white-bearded, white-haired old man in tattered but once ornate robes.

'This way. Quick,' he said.

The Doctor needed no second invitation as he

followed the old man between a gap in the rock face and into another tunnel.

The Creature slapped the rock where the Doctor had just been.

The old man lead the Doctor down a maze of passages, some of which they had to crawl along on hands and knees, so low were the roofs. At last they reached a small cave where they could stand upright. The cave was lit by a couple of small lamps. These were no more than crude terra-cotta shells in which a wick floated on some kind of vegetable oil.

The old man carefully brushed the dirt off his robes. The Doctor was able to see that these were covered in various signs, presumably of some mystic significance.

'Thank you,' said the Doctor, 'for saving me from that thing.'

The old man waved his thanks aside. 'Think nothing of it, my friend. As my dear mother always used to say—she was born under the sign of Pratus, middle cusp,' he observed in passing, 'if you can help somebody, like prevent them from being eaten by a monster, then do so. They might be grateful.'

'Indeed I am,' replied the Doctor. 'Grateful, that is. And to whom must I express my gratitude. Your name, sir?'

'Organon, sir,' declared the old man, drawing himself to his full height and pulling his tattered robes about him. 'Astrologer extraordinary, seer to Princes and Emperors. The Future foretold, the Past explained, the Present apologised for.'

'What brings you here?'

Organon look pained. The memory still rankled. 'A little matter of a slight error in prophecy, sir,' he explained.

The Doctor nodded sympathetically.

'Are you perhaps in the business yourself, sir?' enquired the old man.

The Doctor shrugged modestly. 'Did this prophecy by any chance concern the Lady Adrasta?' he asked.

Organon nodded. 'Ah,' he said, 'you've met her. Very difficult woman.'

The Doctor smiled. 'Difficult' was hardly the word he would have used to describe the Lady Adrasta. Still . . .

'Very literal mind,' complained Organon. 'I mean, when I foretold that she would have visitors who came from beyond the stars, she nearly went beserk. I mean I'm used to creating an effect—I do it rather well,' he confided to the Doctor. 'Use a big dramatic voice. Close my eyes. Spread my arms wide. And say, "I see a creature coming to you from beyond the stars."' Organon's voice boomed impressively in the enclosed space.

'Very good,' said the Doctor admiringly.

Organon smiled with modest satisfaction. 'It's nothing really,' he explained, 'just the result of years of practice. Believe in yourself, my mother used to say, and others will believe in you. Trouble was, the Lady Adrasta didn't. Believe, that is.'

'I think she did,' replied the Doctor.

Organon stared at him incredulously. 'You do? You mean she really thought that I could see something coming from beyond the stars?'

It was more than likely, thought the Doctor. Something had certainly got the Lady Adrasta worried.

'Oh, dear,' said Organon, shaking his head, 'I've done it again, haven't I? I get carried away, you know. It's all right when I stick to astrology; I'm a pretty good astrologer. It's just that sometimes on the spur of the moment I get a sort of urge to ... er ...,' he searched for a suitable word, 'er ... overelaborate. You know how it is?'

The Doctor nodded sympathetically. He knew exactly how it was. It was the story of his own life: overelaboration; never knowing when to stop; always going that bit further even when caution and good sense said you had gone far enough. How much trouble had he got himself in to doing just that? A wise man would know when to call a halt. On the other hand, he reflected, a wise man could get bored out of his mind. Whereas he had always enjoyed himself. It had been interesting. Sometimes even fun.

'That would explain why the Lady Adrasta turned so nasty,' declared Organon. 'She kept asking questions. What sort of creature it was; how big; where it came from; how it travelled. Well, how was I to answer? So I indulged in a little professional ... er ...'

'Vagueness?'

'Discretion. Not that it did me any good,' complained the old man. 'She threw me down here. Do you think she's actually afraid of something coming from beyond the stars?'

5

Organon

As usual the bandits were indulging in their favourite pastime: arguing. They were conducting yet another post mortem over Romana's escape. Who was to blame? Who had allowed Torvin to be struck down by K9's laser?

'Call yourself bandits?' sneered Torvin, who felt the need to establish his ascendancy over them once again, even if only by streams of abuse. He was uneasily aware that so far he had not exactly distinguished himself in this affair. Shift the blame to them: make 'em feel guilty.

'That mechanical animal was made of metal,' he continued. 'Every square centimetre of it. Pure metal. Without a spot of rust on it. There was probably more metal in that thing than we've even managed to steal in four moonflows.'

They looked at their hoard. Once it had seemed to represent untold wealth. But now they saw it for what it was—a pathetic pile of scrap metal, bent, battered, rusty.

'And you let that thing walk out of here!'

'It didn't exactly walk,' objected Ainu, who was always a stickler for accuracy. 'It sort of glided.'

'Walked, glided, flew—what does it matter? The question is why didn't you stop it? And her?'

Ainu scratched his ear, remembering how it had been: the girl calm and contemptuous, her animal bright and deadly. He had the feeling that Torvin had been lucky. If the thing had wanted to kill, they might all be dead by now.

But Torvin wasn't one to give weight to such considerations. In any case he had other matters on his mind. 'You realise what this means, don't you?' he demanded. 'We've got to get packed up. We've got to move. Now.'

'Why?' asked Edu.

'Use your brains,' pleaded Torvin. 'Just this once. Don't let your grey matter congeal like cold porridge between your ears. Think!'

The bandits thought. It was not a process with which they were familiar and they showed signs of strain.

'I still don't see why we have to move,' objected Edu.

Torvin stared at him in despair. 'Because that girl and the animal know where our cave is. Which means they can lead Adrasta's troopers straight here. Do you want to hang around and wait for them?'

The bandits reacted sharply. The prospect of being trapped in the cave by Adrasta's men and a pack of Wolfweeds was anything but reassuring.

'But are you sure she's anything to do with the Lady Adrasta?' protested Edu. 'I got the feeling that she wasn't.'

'Bluff,' declared Torvin. 'You were taken in by her. In any case, dare we risk staying here now you've let her go? Do you imagine that the Lady Adrasta would miss a chance to get her hands on our loot?' he went on. 'There must be two bodyweights of metal here. I bet you at this very moment she's planning an expedition to wipe us out.'

'What are we going to do?' asked the bandits.

In the mind of every great man there comes a moment of revelation, a moment of pure inspiration. Torvin was similarly afflicted. He held his head. It suddenly felt as if it was bursting.

'What are we going to do?' repeated Edu.

Horrified, Torvin heard himself say, 'Attack the Palace!'

The bandits shuffled uneasily. Some were already beginning to edge towards the cave entrance. Had Torvin gone mad? How could they attack the Palace? It was protected by guards and packs of Wolfweeds.

'Adrasta's going to send troops to look for us, isn't she? Which means there'll be fewer guarding the Palace. Right?' demanded Torvin.

The bandits nodded, unhappily aware they were about to be talked into some lunatic plan of action.

'While she's searching for us, do you know where we'll be?'

The bandits tried to think of some hideout safe from guards and Wolfweeds, and failed.

'We'll be inside the Palace sacking Adrasta's own metal vaults. It's the last place they'll expect us to be,' declared Torvin.

For the first time since the bandits had captured Romana they began to smile.

Organon was sitting on a rock and leaning back against the wall of the tunnel. Both hands clasped one knee to his chest, while he expatiated upon the politics and economy of the planet Chloris. He was in fact, as the Doctor discovered, a mine of information.

The astrologer had travelled all over the planet, moving from the court of one petty chieftain to another, scattering horoscopes and prophecies as he went. Not surprisingly he was remarkably shrewd and well informed about the affairs of Chloris. He had to be. To survive at all in the kind of savage society that seemed endemic on the planet was no mean feat. To persuade the various khans and princelings that he alone could interpret the stars that influenced their fate was little short of miraculous. If nothing else, Organon was a survivor. The very fact that he had survived even the Pit and had managed to live cheek by jowl with the Creature said much for his resilience and ingenuity.

'Always leave them happy or bewildered,' observed Organon sagely. 'Ideally the latter. At least that's always been my policy. Leave them feeling as if they've had a revelation of the future—which shouldn't look too depressing, by the way, but should be totally confusing. That way you have time to beat a discreet but dignified retreat before anything too disastrous occurs. It also means that you can return should nothing very serious have happened meanwhile.'

'Doesn't seem to have worked this time,' remarked the Doctor.

'No. I still can't make out what went wrong.'

'How long have you been down here?'

'Two moonflows, I think,' replied the astrologer. 'But that's only a guess. It seems longer. But it's so difficult to keep track of time when you're underground.'

The Doctor nodded sympathetically.

Organon went on to explain how he had managed to survive. He had collected rainwater and water that seeped through the rocks. As for food, some of Lady

Adrasta's serfs had taken to throwing food down the mineshaft—whether as supplies for friends who had been condemned to the Pit or whether they sought to propitiate the Creature, he didn't know. But whatever the reason, whatever the food, it was all greatefully received.

'Does the Creature ever eat it?' asked the Doctor.

'No,' replied Organon. 'Which is curious.'

The Doctor inspected one of the terra-cotta lamps that lit the cave with a smoky light.

'I found these and some oil,' explained the old astrologer. 'They must have been left behind by the miners when the Creature first invaded the mine.'

'Did it?'

'What?'

'Invade the mine?'

'Well,' Organon paused to consider, 'it must have done.'

'Why?'

'It suddenly appeared. At least that's what everyone said.'

'When?'

'I don't know,' confessed the astrologer. 'But it can't have been more than seventeen years ago—because I did this part of the planet then.'

The Doctor could imagine the astrologer years younger in full flood.

'I mean if there had been anything like that thing around in those days, I would have heard. I keep my ears pretty close to the ground, you know.'

'I can imagine,' said the Doctor.

'Anyway it seems to suit the Lady Adrasta.'

The Doctor looked surprised. Organon went on to

explain that since she owned the only successful mine on the planet, the presence of the Creature made metal even scarcer than it was before.

'Most interesting,' said the Doctor.

'Is it?' replied Organon.

'Oh yes. Can't you see a pattern in events?'

The astrologer scratched his head. Patterns were his forte, he admitted. But, when it came to the Lady Adrasta, all he could ever see was trouble.

Trouble in another form was rapidly approaching: a smell like old car batteries; a movement of air in the tunnel; and a sound like nothing the Doctor had ever heard before.

The sound came closer.

'How big is it?' whispered the Doctor.

'Huge,' replied Organon simply. 'Unimaginably huge.'

'That noise it makes ...'

'I sometimes think it's singing,' confessed the astrologer. 'Or weeping. Or else it's in pain. You know,' he went on, 'I've been all over this planet. But I've never heard of another Creature like this. It's unique.'

The Doctor didn't reply. He was staring at something; not a tentacle—you couldn't call it a tentacle. Some kind of projection of the Creature, a livid purulent green, had entered the cave. It probed, like a huge tongue at a tooth cavity feeling blindly for particles of food. Is that all we are to the Creature, wondered the Doctor. Food?

It was done at last. Romana straightened herself tiredly and rubbed her back. Removing the resinous Wolfweed webs that had cocooned K9 had taken a good hour. She had had to scrape them off his body after first soaking them with some kind of oil that Madam Karela had provided.

'Is the tin animal ready yet?' demanded the Lady Adrasta.

'Nearly, my lady.'

'Hurry. I want to see how it works.'

And so you shall, thought Romana, so you shall. If only there's enough energy in his power packs. I'll give you a demonstration you'll never forget. But it all depended on how much the Wolfweed fibres had weakened K9. Romana bent and scraped at the last of the web that still adhered to K9's head.

'K9, can you hear me?' she whispered.

'Mistress,' came the weak reply.

'Do you still have enough power to stun?'

'Affirmative.'

But Madam Karela had noticed the exchange. 'She is whispering to that tin animal,' she informed Adrasta. 'I don't like it. There is treachery afoot.'

Adrasta smiled and beckoned the two guards to stand closer to Romana.

Good, thought Romana. Not so far for K9 to project his ray.

'Well, Romana,' demanded the Lady Adrasta impatiently, 'we are waiting for your demonstrations.'

K9 indicated his readiness for action. Romana picked him up in her arms and turned towards Adrasta and Madam Karela. The guards flinched uneasily and fingered their weapons as they stared down the business end of K9's laser gun.

I've got to knock them out first, thought Romana. No

alternative, otherwise I'll end up with a knife in my ribs before I can deal with the two women.

'Come closer,' she said. 'I'd like you to examine the machine before I switch it on. Don't be afraid. Now, K9!'

K9's laser cut down the two guards. But as it did so, Adrasta and Karela dived for cover behind the throne. At Adrasta's command more guards rushed into the audience chamber. Another went down from the effects of K9's ray, but before Romana could turn the robot animal on to Adrasta the other guards had seized her.

'I want her alive!' screamed Adrasta. She went up and spoke to K9. 'Tin dog, do that again,' she said, 'and my guards will cut your mistress's throat.'

K9's head drooped and his power packs switched off. The guards placed him on a table facing a wall of the audience chamber.

Adrasta smiled at Romana, who was struggling, held by two guards.

'Excellent, my dear,' she observed. 'An invaluable demonstration. I was sure the mechanical creature was a killing machine. Thank you for proving it to me. I have a task for him. I have need of such a killing machine.'

The Doctor and Organon flattened themselves against the walls of the cave as the club-shaped projection of the Creature probed carefully, delicately into every crevice of the rock face. The Doctor stared at the texture of the Creature's skin. It reminded him of something, but what? Close to it didn't look slimy at all. He had the impression that if he touched it it would feel as dry as old leaves.

Just as he was about to discover the precise texture of the probe which was waving gently, almost hypnotically, in front of his face, Organon acted. The astrologer seized one of the terra-cotta lamps, in which a lighted wick floated on a small quantity of vegetable oil, and thust the naked flame against the Creature.

For a long moment nothing happened. The skin in the area of the flame bunched into nodules like stubby proto-fingers. They tested the flame, tried to grasp it. The Doctor watched the skin around the nodules blacken. Then suddenly the miniature projections disappeared and were absorbed into the Creature, which then slowly withdrew from the cave.

Organon chuckled delightedly. 'Didn't like that, did it? Bet it won't come back here again in a hurry.'

The Doctor wasn't so sure. He found it hard to believe that a burned finger would deter the creature. Still, it was always useful to know that it was sensitive to heat. How sensitive, he wasn't sure. Had they hurt the Creature? Did it actually feel pain?

'What sign were you born under?' enquired Oganon. 'Aquatrion?* Caprius? Ariel? If only I had my charts here, I bet we would have discovered that this was your lucky day. Or perhaps it was mine. That's one thing I can never forgive the Lady Adrasta for: throwing me down here without my astrological charts. How can one possibly plan anything?'

*Precise comparisons between Chlorisian astrology and classical Terran astrology are not possible. Chloris circles its sun in 427 Earth days, and the Chlorissian Zodiac contains seventeen houses. Aquatrion is the third house, Caprius the ninth, Ariel the fourteenth and Pratus, mentioned earlier, the fifteenth.

'Did you examine that thing's skin?' asked the Doctor.

'Can't say I did. I was more concerned in trying to keep it from examining mine.'

'Cerebral membrane!'

Organon looked blank.

'The membrane that protects the brain!' declared the Doctor excitedly. 'That's what that thing's skin looked like.'

'You mean the Creature is just a huge brain? But it can't be.'

'Why not?' demanded the Doctor.

'Well, where's the rest?' asked the bewildered astrologer. 'Arms? Legs? Body? Skull, even?'

'It doesn't need them,' explained the Doctor. 'Just think of it: an enormous brain covered with a sensitive motor membrane, so it can move about, but no unnecessary appendages, no bones to break, no muscles to strain. Very practical if you think about it. And from the evolutionary viewpoint, absolutely fascinating.'

But Organon was not impressed. He found the Creature anything but fascinating: frightening, yes; fascinating, no. He had always thought of the thing as a kind of giant bag of slime. Oddly enough, that was a more comforting thought; slime was somehow something one could cope with. But several hundred tons of animated grey matter oozing along the tunnels of the mine was a distinctly unnerving prospect.

A thought occurred to him. 'It can't be a brain,' he objected, 'It's green, not grey. You can't have a green brain.'

'Why not?'

Organon couldn't think of an immediate answer, but a further objection to the Doctor's thesis had struck him.

'It hasn't got a mouth,' he declared. 'So how does it eat? Tell me that.'

'I don't know,' replied the Doctor. 'Let's find out. Come on!'

Suddenly Organon could think of a dozen good reasons why they should not find out. For one thing he could be wrong. Suppose the Creature did have a mouth. He had been known to be wrong before. In fact, come to think of it, he had frequently been wrong about horoscopes and prophecies, and they were his speciality. Until now he had never been expected to provide practical proof.

'I don't think so, if you don't mind,' he said. 'I don't think I'll ...'

But the Doctor had gone after the Creature.

He's mad, Organon told himself. Nice fellow but quite, quite mad. You can't go up to some sabre-toothed monster and ask it if it's a carnivore. There is only one way it can prove it is: it eats you. Satisfied with his argument, he sat back on a rock and contemplated his lamp. The cave seemed to close around him—cold, inhospitable and lonely. 'Hey, wait for me!' cried Organon.

He caught up with the Doctor in the tunnel leading to what he had long ago decided was the Creature's lair. 'I decided to come after all,' he informed the Doctor. 'You might need help.'

'I probably will,' replied the Doctor. 'Thanks. It's just up ahead,' he added.

Organon froze. He stared into the blackness ahead.

'What I can't understand,' observed the Doctor, 'is what a creature like that is doing down here. Pure brain, hundreds of feet in length, trapped at the bottom of a pit, oozing around like so much animated jelly, and sitting on whoever it finds: where's the intellectual stimulation in that? It's not much of a life for the biggest brain in the universe, is it?'

'Who can read such mysteries?' replied Organon. 'Perhaps that is its fate. Perhaps it is all written in the stars.'

'Perhaps it was born amongst them.'

6

The Web

Madam Karela had tied the knots as tightly as she knew how. Romana couldn't move at all. The bands cut into her wrists and ankles. The gag the old woman had stuffed into her mouth was choking her. Every so often the evil old woman pricked her throat with her knife.

Meanwhile Adrasta was interrogating K9, who, under the threat of his mistress's immediate demise, was proving to be a mine of information. In fact he was opening her eyes to a whole new world of possibilities.

'And what do you call this machine in which you travel with Romana and the Doctor?' demanded Adrasta.

'The TARDIS. It stands for Time And Relative Dimensions in Space.'

'You mean you travel through space and time in it?'

'Affirmative.'

Space and Time, thought Adrasta. New worlds are at last opening up to me. I hold the key in my hand—or at least this damned metal animal does.

'You realise what this means?' she said to Karela. 'We can go anywhere, into any time, and bring back what we need: metallic ores, the pure metal itself, slaves—a whole new technology. And I will be the mistress of it all.'

'But we don't know how to operate the TARDIS,' objected Karela.

'The animal does. So does the girl.'

'Beware, my lady,' whispered Karela. 'How can we trust these two creatures? They are not of Chloris.'

'No,' agreed Adrasta. 'But that is why I believe them. They can have no idea why I need their space and time machine. If they did, they would have lied.'

Adrasta regretted the death of the Doctor. He had outmanoueuvred her, it was true, but at the cost of his own life and in order to preserve Romana. A quixotic, sentimental fool of course, but it showed a certain courage. Such a man could have proved useful in her search throughout the universe.

'Perhaps he is not dead,' suggested Karela. 'I know no one ever survives the Pit, but he seemed quite a resourceful man. If he were still alive ...'

Adrasta considered the possibility. Of course it was unlikely in the extreme that he had survived. On the other hand, she could not forget his deliberate plunge into the Pit—even after he had seen the Creature and that fool engineer's death.

'I will take some guards and go down into the Pit and see if he is alive,' volunteered Karela. 'If we are careful, we could avoid the Creature.'

Adrasta made her decision. 'We will all go,' she declared. 'And we'll take that tin animal with us.'

K9 rotated his aural sensors. 'Correction, my lady,' he said, 'I am not made of tin.'

'That thing has been listening to us,' complained Karela. 'It's not to be trusted. Why do we need it?'

'To kill something I should have killed years ago,'

replied Adrasta. 'Something that's too vast for you to cut its throat—even if you could find it.'

The Creature lay in the largest cavern in the mine, hunched, curled miserably in on itself. Through its skin it felt the bars being slid back from the door that led down from the Palace into the mineshaft. It felt the door being opened. It felt the heat from the torches carried by the guards. It smelt or felt the flood of fresh air from above, the sound of many footsteps, and the scent of fear among the guards. It was also aware of the Doctor and Organon moving softly, moving closer.

The Creature was sensitive through its integument to almost every physical and mental stimulus: ultra-violet light, infra-red, gamma-rays, beta-rays, x-rays, sound, touch, heat, cold, thought waves, even gravitational waves. It was aware of so many potential means of communication, yet it was unable to communicate with these ridiculous creatures who moved about on such impractical appendages. Perhaps the possession of such extremeties destroyed their ability or will to communicate.

Part of the Creature slept and dreamed of its home planet: the beautiful orange seas with the long, soft, indigo beaches where it used to laze on pure powdered carbon; the dark red sky above, in which floated great sulphur clouds; and the rain. Oh, how it missed the rain! The warm, sweet, sulphuric acid rain of home.

And then it was suddenly aware of something else: an alien, mechanical intelligence. The thought patterns of K9, who was being carried between two guards, impinged on the Creature's receptors. The Creature stirred uneasily in its dream. Here was danger; here was the unknown. It woke, alert to the movements in the various tunnels.

'Which way now, my lady?' demanded Madam Karela, raising high her torch, which guttered uneasily in the draughts in the tunnel.

The small procession paused. They had come to a junction of four tunnels, each dark and silent except for the occassional drip, drip of water.

Romana was glad of a rest and a chance to flex her fingers. Her wrists were still tied together, while another rope encircled her neck and was held by one of the guards. As they stumbled down the ill-lit passages she was constantly half-throttled.

'Which way, my lady?' repeated Madam Karela.

The Lady Adrasta inspected the mouth of each tunnel. She rubbed the palm of her hand over the wall and held it to her nostrils. The smell was unmistakable: acidic.

'There. That one,' she pointed. 'Send some guards ahead, Guardmaster.'

The Guardmaster, tall and resplendent in his black uniform, ordered three guards to go ahead of him down the tunnel. They cocked the crude harpoon guns they carried.

'Tell them to beware,' she said. 'The Creature is close.'

Unwillingly, but more afraid of the Lady Adrasta's wrath than the Creature, the guards advanced with caution into the darkness. Their torches threw fantastic shadows on the rock face.

The Doctor and Organon were also closing in on the Creature. They moved warily, sensing its vast presence somewhere ahead of them.

'What are we going to do when we find the thing?' whispered Organon.

'I don't know.'

'What?' Organon paused, unable to believe his ears. 'What do you mean you don't know? Haven't you got a plan?'

'Oh, I've got a plan alright,' declared the Doctor. Organon felt somewhat relieved, until his companion added, 'But I've no idea how to carry it out. That's all.'

Organon was about to give vent to the full flow of his invective—which was considerable—when the tunnel curved and they emerged into a huge cavern, large as a cathedral. Obviously the original seam of ore had petered out here and generations of miners had driven galleries and tunnels into the rock face, searching for fresh traces of the metal that was so precious to them. It was like the inside of a honeycomb.

The Creature almost filled the cavern, indeed, more than filled it. Parts of the thing overflowed from holes in the roof and walls. In places it hung down like huge green stalactites. The sheer, unimaginable bulk of the thing took one's breath away.

The Creature lay quiescent, as if asleep. Then one of the stalactites moved slightly.

At that moment Adrasta's party emerged from one of the other tunnels. The guards' immediate reaction was to raise their harpoon guns.

Another stalactite stirred and swung easily in the

darkness about their heads. Delicately, slowly, it extended itself reaching towards where they stood.

Without waiting for orders, terrified by the presence of the Creature, two of the guards fired. Their muskets made a deafening noise in the confined space. Two heavy, serrated wooden harpoons struck the Creature and disappeared into its bulk.

The Creature didn't react. It made no sign of anger or hurt. Then another stalactite extended itself from the roof. It expanded at its tip, like some great paddle and swung towards the guards.

Three more discharged their muskets. Three vicious-looking harpoons struck the Creature, entering its body until they too disappeared from view.

It was Romana who first noticed the Doctor.

'No!' she screamed. 'Don't!'

'Come back!' cried Organon.

But too late. Adrasta and her guards stared, unable to move.

The Doctor was walking up to the Creature. When at last he stood in front of it, with its great mass towering over him, he put out his hand and touched the skin. The skin wasn't slimy; it was dry. He ran his hand across the surface of the Creature. It felt warm, almost velvety.

'Hello there,' said the Doctor. 'My name is ...' But he never had a chance to introduce himself. Because suddenly, with extraordinary speed, the Creature moved. Its vast bulk rolled over him like a tank.

Romana saw the Doctor disappear into a huge tidal wave of green. The wave swept on towards Adrasta and the guards. Nothing seemed able to stop it. The guards reacted instinctively. Some turned to flee. But others readied their harpoon muskets and discharged them into the advancing Creature. Heavy wooden harpoons sank out of sight into the approaching green wall. The cavern echoed with a discharge of muskets. The primitive gun powder created clouds of foul black smoke, which obscured everything and made everyone cough.

When the smoke cleared an extraordinary sight met their eyes. The Creature seemed to be changing colour.

'It's hurt!' cried the Lady Adrasta triumphantly. 'We've wounded it!'

But no blood, green or otherwise, oozed from the Creature. The colour change seemed to be caused by shimmering silver threads which formed on its skin. The threads formed patterns, crossing and criss-crossing each other. The Creature was weaving a web between the guards and itself. It was a web which swiftly grew thicker and more complex—until it was completely filled in. It became a dense, opaque surface, curved like an egg.

Organon and the Guardmaster advanced and gingerly tapped the structure. It was like striking a brick wall, except it was smooth.

'Go on!' commanded Adrasta. 'Break through. Kill the Creature!'

'It's hard as rock, my lady,' replied the Guardmaster. He struck the shell with the hilt of his sword. It made a dull booming sound. 'You'd need a lako* of gunpowder to even scratch it. And even then ...' He shrugged. There was nothing in the available technology of Chloris that could cope with such an obstacle.

'But you must!' cried Romana. 'The Doctor's behind there! We'll have to break through.'

*1 lako is approximately 1¼ tons.

7

The Meeting

A distant booming sounded inside his head, like the sound of waves breaking inside a subterranean cave, or like some savage beating of slow rhythms on a hollowed log. The Doctor groaned and opened his eyes. It was dark—but a darkness lit by traces of failing phosphorescence, on the walls, on the roof.

Suddenly the Doctor sat up, remembering the Creature and what had happened. He had no idea how long he had been unconscious, but at least he was still in one piece, or nearly so. Gingerly he felt his legs. A few bruises perhaps, but no bones broken. His skin tingled as if he had been subjected to a mild charge of static electricity.

Where was the Creature? The Doctor looked round. But the thing had gone. It had vanished, except for traces of phosphorescence which led down one of the tunnels.

The booming noise sounded again. It seemed to be coming from the other side of the extraordinary shell-like structure that sealed off the rest of the cavern. The Doctor scraped at the surface with his penknife. He was astonished to discover that it was metallic.

The shell boomed as if someone was trying to communicate. The Doctor picked up a rock and struck the shell hard.

'It's him!' declared Organon, rubbing his ear vigorously. He had pressed it against the surface of the structure close by where the Doctor was knocking from the other side. The reverberations had almost deafened him.

But the Guardmaster was cautious. 'Maybe it's that thing knocking,' he objected.

'No, no,' snapped Organon. 'It's him, the Doctor. I'd know his knock anywhere. He's alive. Come on. We've got to break this down.' He inspected the point at which the structure joined the rockface. The extraordinary thing was that it seemed almost to grow out of the rock. But logic insisted that was probably where it was weakest.

Led by Ainu, the bandits reached the Palace walls under cover of the jungle. There they paused apparently unnoticed by the guards.

'What do we do now Torvin?' demanded Ainu in a hoarse whisper.

What had seemed such a brilliant plan in the safety of their cave now seemed like suicidal madness. The sight of these massive walls towering twenty or more feet above them, seemingly impervious to any attack, weighed heavily on their spirits. How could they possibly take the Palace? How could they even breach its defences?

Torvin could already hear uneasy mutterings from his men. In a minute he knew they would begin to fade away, like hoarfrost in the sun. He had to think of something. Quickly. Then he saw it—their passport into Adrasta's Palace. 'Ivy!'

'Ivy?' The bandits gazed upwards. It was true that ivy and lianas grew thick on the walls, even reaching as far as the Palace roof. It grew like a pelt on some huge stone beast. The tiny filaments of its root systems found precarious holds in the soft mortar between the stones of the wall.

Ainu seized a thick rope of ivy and pulled hard. A small bat and a scattering of old mortar and brick dust flew out.

'Seems strong enough,' he said without enthusiasm.

'Come on, lads,' whispered Torvin. 'Start climbing. Edu first.'

Edu was the smallest of the miners. Years before, when they worked underground, he had been the one to crawl down the narrowest passages, the man sent to work on the most inaccessible seams of ore. The puka*, they had christened him then. And when his courage had sometimes failed him, they had driven him ahead of them with kicks and curses.

Agile as a monkey, Edu swung up into the ivy. Compared to negotiating galleries no more than a foot high, in total darkness, hundreds of feet underground, climbing ivy was child's play to him. He paused for a moment, then leaned down to Torvin. 'What do I do if I meet a guard?' he asked anxiously.

'Keep him chatting while we climb up and cut his throat,' Torvin instructed. He turned to his followers. 'Come on. Think of all that metal in Adrasta's vaults. They say she has over a thousand bodyweights of copper alone.'

*The puka is a kind of rodent that inhabits the interior of hollow trees on Chloris.

The thought stirred the bandits into action. They seized the ivy by the stems, which were as thick as a man's wrist, and began to ascend.

The guard patrolling the upper battlements of the Palace paused for a moment, listening. He could hear a rustling in the creepers that covered the Palace wall. Was a breeze getting up? No, more likely a sudden activity amongst the birds and rodents and lizard-like creatures that inhabited the thick mat of vegetation. Ignoring the noise, he gazed upwards at the night sky. Above him he could see Chloris's four moons. It was lucky, so they said, when you could see all the moons together. Make a wish. He closed his eyes and wished: to make Guardmaster before he was thirty.

Suddenly he felt something strike him between his shoulder blades. He felt no pain, only a wetness in the middle of his back. He put one hand to the spot and with astonishment touched the protruding handle of a knife. He turned and saw a small, incredibly filthy individual, one leg over the parapet, watching him. Too astonished to cry out, he died where he stood.

The Lady Adrasta tapped the shell-like structure with the back of her hand, her rings making a sound of metal against metal.

Organon and the Guardmaster were still battering away at the point at which the structure joined the rock face. But their efforts had not met with success. Indeed, no matter what tools they used they seemed to be unable to make any impression on the material woven by the Creature.

'Stop that!' ordered Adrasta.

'But my lady, the Doctor is behind there,' objected Organon.

Adrasta ignored him. She stroked the shell, then using the diamond that blazed in one of her rings, tested it on the material. But even the diamond made no impression. The structure woven by the Creature was harder than anything known to Chloris.

'Bring Romana and the animal,' she commanded the Guardmaster.

But Madam Karela was uneasy at the prospect. 'My lady,' she protested, 'it is too dangerous. We do not know what this tin thing might do in conjunction with the Creature. Perhaps they are already in league with each other.'

Adrasta shook her head.

'But we cannot be sure,' declared Madam Karela.

'We know the little animal will not harm its mistress. Particularly if you, Karela, stand with your knife at her throat while the metal animal does our bidding.'

The Guardmaster returned with Romana and a guard carrying K9.

Adrasta came straight to the point. 'As you know, the Doctor is trapped behind this,' she said, tapping the shell. 'He's in there with the Creature. He may be alive or dead. We cannot be sure.'

'He's alive,' declared Organon stoutly. 'I've heard him tapping.'

'In which case,' continued Adrasta, 'all the more reason to hurry.' She turned to Romana. 'My dear, I thought K9 could help. Have you enough power to pierce the shell, K9?'

K9 did not reply. He was programmed not to answer the questions of enemies.

'Tell her,' ordered Romana.
'Impossible to answer the question,' replied K9. 'First I will have to evaluate the molecular structure of the material which I am required to pierce. Then I must compute the power needed to create sufficient molecular stress ...'
'Evaluate, little animal,' snapped Adrasta. 'Compute.'
Romana told the guard to put K9 down. K9 rolled forward and, like any normal dog, put his nose to the shell.

The Doctor struck a match which flared in the darkness. The tunnel ahead was empty. There was no sound, no movement of air. The match scarcely flickered in his hand. Cautiously he began to make his way down the tunnel, following the traces of phosphorescence which clung to the walls showing where the Creature had passed. It is leaving a trail, thought the Doctor. I wonder why. It is almost as if it wanted me to follow.
His foot struck a piece of metal. He bent and picked it up. As he did so, the match flickered and died. But what he had seen was enough to make him scrabble in his pocket for more matches. Yes, it was unmistakeable. As a fresh match burst with light, the Doctor found himself staring at a small piece of pure cadmium.
He looked at the tunnel walls, studying the strata. There was no doubt about it, the cadmium didn't come from here. In fact he doubted if there were any workable cadmium deposits on the planet. So where did it come from?
A pace further ahead another piece of metal gleamed. This time it was a nugget of manganese. More pieces of

metal, each different, each unadulterated by any impurities, lay ahead.

He was kneeling, examing a piece of iron when he sensed a movement ahead. The match in his hand flickered out. But the light increased—the unmistakeable green light which emanated from the Creature.

He looked up to see the Creature oozing (there was no other way to describe its motions) round a bend in the tunnel. It paused a few yards from him.

After his previous experience the Doctor approached the thing with the utmost caution. The moment it moved, its skin rippling almost as if in fear or exhaustion, the Doctor stopped.

'Friend. Friend,' he kept repeating. I hope you understand me, he thought. I hope you know what friend means. But how do you communicate with a gigantic green blob that is without eyes or ears? 'Look I'm not armed,' he said. 'I won't hurt you.' How could I hurt something that seems to have no organs of sense at all? Where is its vulnerable spot? How could you even start to find it in that enormous bulk?

Now close to the Creature, the Doctor stroked the skin, watching a network of what appeared to be veins pulsing with a green light. Green blood? But surely one only found such a thing in creatures like caterpillars that lived off green plants. A worrying thought occurred to him; suppose this was just the larva of some huge insect.

Curiosity overcoming caution for a moment, he reached out to touch the Creature's skin. The skin recoiled before his hand. 'It's all right,' murmured the Doctor, patting the Creature as if soothing a nervous horse. 'It's all right. Don't be frightened.' His attentions seemed to calm the Creature. 'Good boy. Or good girl, as the case may be.'

Perhaps it communicated by telepathy or some form of thought transference. On a sudden impulse the Doctor placed his head against the green skin of the Creature. He closed his eyes and concentrated on projecting peaceful thoughts of friendship.

The Creature remained motionless. It didn't react in any way. The Doctor deliberately emptied his mind inviting some reaction. But there was none.

'How do you communicate?' asked the Doctor, stepping back and scratching his head. 'How do you communicate with your own kind? You can't be the only Creature like you in the entire Universe. Surely somewhere, on some planet, there are others like you, aren't there?'

As if in answer, part of the Creature's skin suddenly elongated itself into a huge fist-like projection. It grabbed the Doctor round the throat and bore him to the ground.

'Easy, easy,' gasped the Doctor, struggling to release the hold on his windpipe. 'You're throttling me. You don't know your own strength.' The blood pounded in his ears. He could feel himself beginning to black out. The pressure on his throat became unbearable as the Creature turned him face down on the floor. Then just as swiftly as it had seized the Doctor, it released him. He found himself able to breathe again.

The 'fist' that had gripped changed shape. It elongated into a delicate tendril which began to move in the dirt on the tunnel floor.

The Doctor sat up and rubbed his throat. He watched the tendril tracing some kind of design.

It was a picture. The Creature was drawing a picture of

some kind of shield. There was something familiar about the object. The Doctor knew he had seen it before. But where? Then it came to him. The Creature was drawing the strange shield which hung on the wall of Lady Adrasta's audience chamber.

8

The Shield

Edu put one hand over the guard's mouth to prevent him from crying out. With his other hand he held onto the man's sword arm, so that he could not draw his weapon. At the same time Ainu, using both hands, drove his knife up under the guard's ribs from the front. The knife point grated on bone. The man gave a peculiar sigh and sagged in Edu's grasp. Ainu withdrew his knife and the dead guard slid to the floor, his metal skullcap rolling across the flagstones.

Torvin stepped over the corpse and retrieved the skull cap. He tapped it against the edge of a table. 'Pure metal,' he announced knowledgably. 'Lucky fellow to be able to afford head protection like this. I expect it was a family heirloom.' He put the skullcap into his sack and looked around for more booty.

So far their raid on the Lady Adrasta's Palace had been singularly unproductive. A sword, a couple of knives and a buckler was the extent of their booty. All metal, it is true, but hardly worth the risk and not what Torvin had promised them. They had still not found Adrasta's vaults. But when they entered the audience chamber their eyes lit up. Metal!

The two large candlesticks which flanked Adrasta's throne looked like bronze. They scratched at them experimentally with their knives. Yes, no doubt about it:

bronze. Ainu laid claim to a heavy metal tray which stood on a table. There was also a brass urn and a pewter flagon. Even the door handles and hinges were bronze. The bandits set to to remove them. Only Edu was staring preoccupied at the wall. 'What's that?' he asked, pointing to the shield-like object which the Doctor had noticed the first time he had entered the audience chamber.

Torvin was trying to fit one of the large candlesticks into his sack. 'Bring it over here,' he said, 'and let's see.'

Edu stood on a stool and reached for the shield. The moment he touched it it began to glow, as if lit from within.

'It's hot!' he exclaimed, releasing the shield instantly.

'I don't care if it's on fire,' snapped Torvin. 'Bring it here. And quick!' Already he could hear shouts from the corridor and the sound of running feet. Obviously the corpse of one of the guards they had killed had been found. At any moment Adrasta's men would burst in on them. It was not a prospect Torvin cared to contemplate. He had no illusions about the fighting qualities of his men. Faced with well-trained, well-armed troopers seeking to avenge the deaths of their comrades, he knew that his small band of ex-miners stood little chance. He looked around the audience chamber and realised there was only one exit. They were trapped.

'They're coming!' shouted Ainu from the doorway.

'Barricade the door!'

While his men dragged furniture against the door to prevent the guards from breaking it down, Torvin considered the situation. Tales of the Lady Adrasta's cruelty and cunning were legendary. He found it difficult to believe that she would ever leave herself with only one exit from her audience chamber. Surely there had to be a hidden door or a secret passage somewhere.

The guards began to batter on the door with their sword hilts. Torvin could hear the guard commander calling for a battering ram to be brought. He knew he only had a few minutes in which to find the way out of the audience chamber.

A huge wall-hanging, embroidered with improbable hunting scenes and dating from the reign of the Lady Adrasta's predecessor, caught his eye. Desperately he tore it down. Hidden behind the hanging was a small door heavily barred and bolted. Torvin struggled with the bolts. At last it swung open to reveal a flight of stone steps descending into darkness. His nostrils caught the unmistakeable stale smell of the mine.

'Come on!' he cried. 'This way.'

Edu pointed to the shield. 'What about that?' he asked.

Mentally Torvin compared its weight to that of the candlestick in his sack. The shield, or whatever it was, looked heavier. It was made of a metal he had never seen before. Perhaps it was valuable. 'Give it to me,' he told Edu. 'You take my sack.' Thankfully Edu handed over the shield.

Ignoring the shouts of the guards, Torvin stared at his distorted reflection in the surface of the stange metal. Edu was right: it was warm to the touch. And the thing glowed as if lit by some soft inner light. The glow filled him, soothed him: he felt at peace.

The crash of the battering ram against the door awoke Torvin from his trance. Tucking the shield under his arm, he ran for the door that lead down into the mine. He swung it closed just as the guards burst into the room.

The Doctor stared blankly at the drawing the Creature

had made in the dust of the tunnel floor. He had last seen the shield-like shape hanging on the wall of Adrasta's audience chamber. But what did the Creature want with it? What was it trying to say to him? 'What is it?' he asked the Creature. 'Is it yours? Do you want me to get it for you?'

The Creature retired a few yards down the tunnel, where it suddenly became immobile. Its colour faded. Only faint pulses of green light flashed in its veins (if they were veins). It was as if it had just switched itself off.

'Well, don't just sit there,' complained the Doctor. 'What do you want me to do with this thing? Just supposing it is what I think it is and I did manage to get hold of it.'

But there was no response. The Creature seemed to have sunk into a torpor.

'Give me a clue,' begged the Doctor. 'Anything.'

It was obvious that that was as much explaining as the Creature was prepared to do—or perhaps it had communicated as much as it could. It was hard to know.

With the Creature apparently torpid and uninterested in any further communication, the Doctor began to explore the other tunnels and galleries. In some of these he met other parts of the Creature, which had oozed through small linking passages in the rock.

In one cave he found a large pile of shell-like material, fragments similar to the huge broken eggshell which he and Romana had found at the Place of Death.

As the Doctor began to poke about amongst the fragments, his arm was gripped by a long green tendril which entered from the main passage. Gently the tendril tugged at him, pulling him away from the pieces of shell. When he tried to free himself, a second tendril appeared and wrapped itself round his waist. The Doctor found himself escorted out of the cave.

'All right, all right,' protested the Doctor. 'I can take a hint. So you don't want me to meddle with those fragments. I wonder why.'

The tendril propelled him back into the main cavern, where it suddenly disengaged itself and snaked swiftly back to where the main body of the Creature lay.

'One of these days, my friend,' said the Doctor to the departing tendrils, 'you're going to have a lot of explaining to do.'

'Evaluation complete, mistress,' announced K9 backing away from the shell.

'Does that mean he knows what it's made of?' Adrasta asked Romana.

'Correct, madam,' replied the robot. 'The shell or web—it is difficult to know which would be the correct description—is a complex substance. It is composed of living cells, of a type I have never encountered before, coated with various metallic alloys and held together in one impervious ...'

But Romana was in no mood for a lecture, and she could see that Adrasta wanted straight answers. 'K9, can you break through the shell?' she asked. 'Or web?' she hastily added.

There was silence for a long moment while K9's information banks completed the evaluation. 'I am not yet at full power,' K9 observed, 'owing to the damage sustained whilst under Wolfweed attack.'

'Try,' pleaded Romana. 'The Doctor is behind there.'

Obediently the robot turned to face the shell. The

others stood back and watched as a ray flashed from K9's muzzle onto the strange structure.

Weighed down by their booty, the bandits hastened as fast as they could down the winding stone steps. Fear of the guards behind them drove them on. Soon they entered a maze of narrow passages carved out of the living rock. The passages sloped downwards leading them ever deeper under ground.

Torvin was delighted. 'What a haul!' he kept repeating. 'What a haul! Did you ever see such a haul?'

He carried the shield in his arms. It continued to glow. Indeed it began to pulse with light. Thanks to this luminescence they had no need of torches and were thus able to make all speed through the winding passages. Behind them, in the distance, they could hear the shouts and curses of Adrasta's guards as they too traversed the tunnels leading down to the mine.

The shield not only glowed with light it was also warm to the touch. Its warmth permeated Torvin's body and mind, a relaxed lazy warmth, the warmth of sunlit summer days. He felt as if he were walking in a dream. All fear had gone from him. When they came to a point where the tunnel divided and Ainu demanded which way they should go, Torvin felt a mild astonishment. It wasn't his decision; it was the shield's. Without reply he took the right-hand fork. Uneasily the others followed.

For several minutes K9 had been directing his ray onto the shell. With the result that a circle about a foot in diameter glowed redly. But the rest of the shell was unaffected. When the robot switched off his ray, even the redness vanished in a matter of seconds.

'What's wrong, K9?' asked Romana anxiously.

But before he could reply Adrasta demanded why he had stopped trying to break through the shell.

'I am in danger of depleting my power packs,' he replied.

The Lady Adrasta, however, was not impressed. 'So far you've had no effect whatsoever,' she observed.

'Incorrect,' declared K9. 'I weakened the shell, but the material is self-renewing and increases in strength.'

Adrasta gazed blankly at Romana. 'What does the little tin animal mean?' she demanded.

'He means that whenever the shell is weakened, the atoms recombine—the molecules reconstitute themselves—to form an even stronger material,' explained Romana.

'So that all he has succeeded in doing is to temper the original material?'

Romana was forced to admit that this was true.

'What use is the little animal to me then?' demanded Adrasta. Her expression grew savage. 'Destroy him.'

'No!' cried Romana, interposing herself between K9 and Adrasta's guards. 'If you damage him again, you'll have destroyed your only defence against the Creature.'

'How can the tin animal kill the Creature when it can't even break the shell?'

The question was unanswerable. And while Romana was trying to think of a reply, the Lady Adrasta turned to her guards once more. 'Destroy the thing,' she commanded. 'He has failed me.'

But before the men could implement her order, the shell suddenly split open apparently of its own accord. It split neatly down the middle, making an opening a couple of feet wide. Through the opening stepped the Doctor.

'Hello,' he said cheerfully.

There are moments, thought Romana, when I positively loathe that man. How dare he look so cheerful when he's been trapped the far side of that shell with a huge ravening what-ever-it-is? How dare he appear looking as if he's just returned from a five-mile hike, when, by the rules that govern the Universe, he should have been torn limb from limb or squashed flatter than a crêpe suzette by a million tons* of green blob?

The Doctor looked from one to the other in some perplexity. For some reason he had the distinct impression that his reappearance was not universally popular. Really people were most extraordinary. Why, even Romana looked miffed. Yes, miffed—that was the word.

'How did you get out of there?' demanded Adrasta.

'Just tapped on the shell and asked old thingummybob to let me out,' replied the Doctor, whose explanation of events was not wholly reliable. In fact he was as surprised as everyone else when the shell split. On the other hand, it was never wise to admit to someone like the Lady Adrasta that one was not totally in charge of events.

Organon seemed to be the only one genuinely pleased to see him. 'I wish I had my star charts and projections with me,' the Astrologer whispered. 'You must have been born under a singularly harmonious and unique conjunction of celestial influences. Everything seems to be going your way today.'

*A pardonable exaggeration under the circumstances: the Creature weighed only 385 tons.

But if the expression on the Lady Adrasta's face was anything to go by, the Doctor wasn't so sure. Adrasta was definitely suspicious of him.

'Why didn't the Creature kill you?' she asked. 'It should have killed you. It killed everyone else who got close to it.'

'Good point,' agreed the Doctor.

'Give me a good answer.'

For once the Doctor was at a loss for words. The question was one that had been puzzling him. Why hadn't the Creature killed him? It could have done; it had had every chance. In fact any self-respecting man-eater would have masticated him within five minutes of their meeting. Unless ...

'Unless it doesn't mean to kill people,' he said at last.

The Lady Adrasta stared at him as if he were insane. 'Then how do you explain all those deaths over the past fifteen years?' she demanded. 'Heart failure?'

'Some of them,' agreed the Doctor. 'After all, it's not the pleasantest of experiences to come face to face with a thing like that, I can assure you. But that's not all. Suppose the Creature has never had anything to do with the human race before. Suppose there are no *homo sapiens* where it comes from. So it doesn't realise what a very fragile species we are. It doesn't realise, for instance, that if you block up our mouths and nostrils we suffocate. If you roll a few hundred tons of green blob over us, we are apt to resemble a Terran tortilla.'

A further thought struck him. 'Suppose,' he continued, 'that where this Creature comes from they don't communicate as we do. Or by telepathy as they do on Argos 2. Or by means of odours as they do on Tau Ceti 13. Or by electrical discharges. Or by anything of that nature. Suppose they communicate directly through their skins. One green blob rolls up to another green blob; they lean against each other, and natter away twenty to the dozen. That would explain why the thing keeps crushing people. All it's doing is trying to be friendly.'

But the Lady Adrasta was not impressed by the Doctor's reasoning. 'It still doesn't explain why it didn't crush you,' she observed.

'Perhaps because I tried to communicate with it.'

'Did you succeed?'

Remembering the drawing the Creature had made in the dirt on the floor of the tunnel, the Doctor prevaricated.

'Not so's you'd notice,' he replied.

Adrasta turned to Madam Karela. 'Take some guards and her,' pointing to Romana, 'and the little tin animal, and go and kill the Creature,' she ordered.

'No!' protested the Doctor. 'You mustn't.'

'Afraid for your green slimy friend?'

'Afraid for them. You have no conception of the power of that Creature.'

'Then why can't it get out of the Pit by itself?' sneered Adrasta.

The Guardmaster was the first one to step through the split in the shell. He looked around and then beckoned the others to follow him. Holding their torches high and with swords drawn they followed him into the darkness beyond. Karela and Romana, with two guards, brought up the rear. Romana carried K9 in her arms.

'Remember, I shall kill you if that tin animal doesn't obey my orders,' said the old woman, pricking Romana none too gently with her knife.

Romana did not reply.

'They haven't a chance against that thing,' protested the Doctor. 'And even if they did succeed in wounding it, it could go beserk and kill us all.'

'Be silent!' snapped Adrasta, staring into the tunnel beyond the shell, where the light from the torches cast grotesque shadows. These faded into blackness as the party proceeded cautiously down the tunnel.

Adrasta, Organon, the Doctor and the remaining guards waited uneasily. They strained their ears for some sound that would indicate that Karela's party had found the Creature. But they heard nothing. The silence was tangible. Minutes passed on leaden feet.

'What's going on behind there?' demanded the Lady Adrasta in a whisper. 'What do you suppose has happened to them?'

The Doctor, who was growing increasingly worried himself, suggested that he go and see. But Adrasta had no intention of letting him out of her sight; she didn't trust him.

'You go,' she ordered Organon.

'Me?' objected the astrologer. He offered a dozen excellent arguments as to why he was quite the wrong choice for such an honour. He was too old, ill, claustrophobic, an abject coward, totally unreliable. He needed time to cast his horoscope, her horoscope, the Creature's horoscope.

Fortunately Madam Karela and the others returned before Organon was forced to choose between immediate execution by the Lady Adrasta's guards or the dubious honour of death via the Creature.

'The Creature's gone, my lady,' declared Karela. 'There's no sign of it.'

'Gone? Where?'

The Doctor informed Adrasta that that meant there was a gigantic green blob loose somewhere in the tunnels of the mine. 'What's more,' he added, 'it's an angry green blob because you tried to have it killed.'

But Adrasta was past reason. 'Take more guards!' she screamed. 'Take K9! Search the whole mine. The Tythonian must be somewhere.'

'The Tythonian?' queried the Doctor. 'Do you mean to say that thing is a Tythonian? Well, well, well. You have bitten off more than you can chew, haven't you?'

Romana edged over to the Doctor. 'What's a Tythonian?' she whispered.

'I've no idea,' the Doctor whispered back. 'But it seems to scare Adrasta.'

The Lady Adrasta looked around her forces and suddenly picked on Romana, who still held K9 in her arms. 'You'll do it,' she said. 'Take K9 and kill the Creature.'

Romana was about to protest, when the Doctor diplomatically intervened. 'Better do your hair first,' he advised. 'You can't go killing anything with your hair all messed up like that.'

Romana stared at him in astonishment. It was the first time he had ever expressed any concern about her coiffeur. 'My hair?' she asked.

'Your hair,' declared the Doctor, producing a mirror from his pocket. 'It looks a fright. Here, take a look at yourself in the mirror.'

Bewildered, Romana stared into the hand mirror. The Doctor seemed to be holding it at a peculiar angle. She couldn't see herself in it. All she could see was the furious and worried face of Adrasta. 'I can't see,' she objected.

'It's just a question of angle,' explained the Doctor. 'I think it's just about right now.'

Romana realised that the Doctor was lining up the mirror for K9, so that he could have a shot at Adrasta. The mirror would reflect the beam from his laser. She eased K9 into a better position.

'That's right,' said the Doctor, pleased that she had guessed his plan so quickly.

Romana lined up K9 on the mirror. 'Ready', she said.

A guard approached the Lady Adrasta seeking orders. He had heard footsteps in the tunnels descending from the Palace. Adrasta turned to speak to him just as K9 fired. The guard was cut down by K9's ray reflected from the mirror held by the Doctor. A second and third guard dropped. Adrasta took to her heels, followed by Madam Karela, and the rest of the guards.

As Romana swung round, K9 cradled in her arms, she saw Adrasta disappearing down one of the tunnels. She tried another shot with the robot's laser. Shards of rocks sprayed from the rock face, just behind where Adrasta's head had been a moment before.

'No!' cried the Doctor. 'No, Romana. We might need him for our own defence.'

He had glimpsed somewhere down the tunnel a green shape. The last thing he wanted was a furious Tythonian (whatever that might be) to come charging into the cavern determined to wreak vengeance on whoever was there.

9

Erato

Fifteen years ago Torvin had known every gallery and tunnel of the mines. With the rest of the miners and pit-boys he had hacked at the rock face, following seams of mineral ore that sooner or later always seemed to peter out. Fifteen years ago he had known these mines as well as the contents of his own wallet. Now he walked these same tunnels and galleries like a sleepwalker, holding the glowing shield in his arms, obedient to its every change of direction. Like a compass, the shield lead him deeper and deeper into the mine. The warmth from the shield suffused him, dulling his brain, reducing him and the other ex-miners to mere automata. No one protested any more; no one even spoke. Wordlessly, obediently, they followed the directions of the glowing shield.

Suddenly the miners entered the cavern. The Creature moved swiftly towards the ex-miners.

Torvin held out the shield with both arms. An indentation appeared in the Creature's skin. Torvin fitted the shield into the indentation and stepped back.

The shield glowed for a moment like a jewel in the skin of the Creature, then it lost its luminosity. The shield became dull. The Creature waited, a black metallic jewel in its skin.

Torvin and the other ex-miners emerged from their

dream. They stared around, appalled to find themselves in the presence of the Creature. 'We're for it now,' declared Edu with gloomy satisfaction.

But the others weren't listening; they were staring at the Doctor who was walking gingerly up to the Creature. He studied the shield which the Creature now wore. Somehow it didn't look like a shield at all now. The boss in the centre had more the appearance of a handle.

On a sudden inspiration the Doctor put out his hand and grasped this handle. An extraordinary tingling sensation in his fingers made him release the shield almost immediately. But not before he had said, 'Sorry.' The Doctor rubbed his hand and stared at the shield in astonishment.

Romana broke the silence. 'Are you all right, Doctor?' she asked.

The Doctor did not reply. Instead he grasped the shield again. This time there was only the faintest of tingles in his finger tips, a sensation almost of pins and needles, but nothing more.

'Hello,' said the Doctor, immediately releasing the shield once again.

'What did you say?' asked the Doctor, staring at the shield.

Romana, puzzled, didn't know what to make of this. Who on earth was he talking to? 'Is there anything wrong?' she asked.

The Doctor scratched his head uncertainly; he seemed bewildered. 'I don't know,' he replied. 'That's to say, either I'm going insane or something very odd is happening.'

'What?'

The Doctor didn't reply and once again took hold of the shield. 'I realise this must be a very frightening experience for you,' declared the Doctor. 'But please don't be alarmed.' The Doctor released his hold on the shield and turned to the others. 'Did you hear what I just said?' he asked.

They nodded.

'Well, I didn't say it,' observed the Doctor.

'Look,' said Romana soothingly, 'I know all this has been very trying for you, but you must keep a grip on yourself. This is no time to crack up.'

'I'm not cracking up!' snapped the Doctor. 'All I'm saying is that I didn't say what I just said.' Then realising that as a statement of fact it verged on the opaque, if not the downright obscure, he tried again. 'Do you remember what I said?'

'You said that you realised this must be a very frightening experience for you, but don't be alarmed.'

The Doctor beamed at her. 'Precisely. That's exactly what I did say. Only I didn't say it. I was too busy being frightened and alarmed to say anything.'

Organon and Romana looked at each other worriedly. The astrologer shrugged. 'Stress affects some people that way,' he whispered to her. 'Perhaps if the Doctor sat down for a bit. Rest works wonders.'

Romana decided to make one more try. 'If you didn't say what you said you said,' she asked, 'who did? Does that make sense?' she enquired of Organon.

'I'm not sure. I'm still trying to work it out.'

The Doctor didn't comment on this. Instead he was examining the shield set like a jewel in the Creature's forehead—if a huge green blob could be said to have such a thing. Gingerly he took hold of the handle in the centre of the shield once again.

'Please allow me to explain,' said the Doctor. 'This is not the Doctor speaking. I am simply using his larynx. We Tythonians are fortunate to have avoided such evolutionary cul-de-sacs. Normally we communicate through our skins. So much more meaningful, I always think, don't you? But then you probably don't, since your skins are capable of processing only the most rudimentary information.'

The Doctor released the shield and felt his throat. 'It feels most peculiar,' he explained, 'someone else using your vocal cords.'

'What's whatsitsname's name?' asked the ever practical Romana.

'Erato,' said the Doctor, when the Creature was once more able to speak through him. 'Like all Tythonians, I have 135 names, indicating clan, family, parents, credit rating, political persuasion, etc. However, when dealing with species whose life cycle is of such indecent brevity, I prefer to use only a single name. You may therefore call me Erato. I am the Tythonian Ambassador to this benighted planet.'

'Then what are you doing skulking around down here in the Pit?' demanded Romana, who found the Tythonian infuriatingly pompous.

'Me? Skulking!' cried the Doctor. 'I am not skulking. Tythonians cannot skulk. We are too large to skulk.'

'Then what are you doing down here?'

'That cunning woman, the Lady Adrasta,' the Doctor explained, 'enveigled me down into this disgusting place and left me here to die. I didn't of course. Tythonians don't very often—die, that is,' he added. 'But she had no means of knowing that. It is dark, damp and uncomfortable down here. I would like to get out.'

But Romana was not convinced. 'Look. If you're not skulking,' she demanded, 'why have you been eating people?'

The Doctor's face went purple in alarm as his voice rose two full octaves in sheer indignation. 'I haven't!' he snapped. 'Eating people is a disgusting habit. We Tythonians live by ingesting mineral salts and chlorophyll through our skin. We do not eat meat.'

The Doctor removed his hand from the shield and ruefully rubbed his Adam's apple. 'Don't make him angry,' he begged in a hoarse whisper. 'It's hell on the throat when he gets worked up.'

'Sorry, Doctor,' said Erato more calmly, when the Doctor risked his larynx once more. 'I do apologise. One tends to forget that whilst we Tythonians arrived at evolutionary perfection many aeons ago, you ape-descended creatures have barely got your foot on the first rung of the evolutionary ladder.'

Romana acidly enquired if the Tythonian was ever going to get to the point. He had not yet explained his presence on Chloris. If he was not there to eat assorted astrologers, for what purpose had he been sent from Tythonus?

'I was on a trading mission to this unfortunate planet. I came here with a treaty which we on Tythonus have been considering for several hundred Chlorissian years. We believe it to be mutually beneficial to both our planets.' At great length and in rolling periods, reminiscent of Macaulay at his worst, the Creature explained the intricacies of the proposed treaty. How, in exchange for chlorophyll, which the Tythonians were prepared to produce themselves from the jungles of

Chloris should it transpire that the state of Chlorissian technology prove inadequate to the task, they would pay in return a generous amount of mineral ore: iron, manganese, copper, gold, platinum, cobalt—whatever was required.

Having discovered the use of the Doctor's voice, the Creature obviously had every intention of enjoying its sound. Until the Doctor broke the connection and asked a question himself. Why did the Tythonians need the chlorophyll now, rather than several hundred years ago?

Suddenly Erato became evasive. When the Doctor seized the shield again, Erato did not answer. The Doctor repeated the question. Eventually the Tythonian was forced to explain.

It seemed that Tythonians lived for about forty thousand Chlorissian years—longer, if they avoided any physical activity, like movement or worry, and devoted themselves exclusively to music and poetry. During their life span there arrived one moment when they could reproduce themselves. This involved a lengthy and fairly complex operation, once two Tythonians (who are essentially tri-sexual) decided to amalgamate. They rolled together, and over the course of a couple of hundred Chlorissian years they absorbed each other, becoming a single enormous entity (probably one mile in length) possessed of no fewer than six different sexes. This entity, this double Tythonian, then gestated for about two thousand Chlorissian years (sometimes longer), and, in the fullness of time, split and produced two identical Tythonians, approximately six inches in length. There were frequent multiple births—triplets or quadruplets. These Tythonian young were for the first two or three hundred years of their life fed on a mixture of chlorophyll, sulphuric acid, and a rare combination of mineral salts found only on the shores of the Orange Sea of Tythonus.

Unfortunately for the future of the race, there were never more than sixty-three fertile Tythonians capable of child-bearing at any one time. Some of those would decide to devote their lives to music or poetry or just lying around and chatting about this and that. The survival of each generation of Tythonian young, therefore, was of paramount importance. But without a steady supply of chlorophyll they were doomed to an early death.

Tythonus, Erato explained, whilst undoubtedly the most beautiful planet in any galaxy, with its red skies and yellow sulphuric acid clouds and indigo beaches, was not rich in vegetation. In fact there was no vegetation left at all—just millions and millions of hectares of gently rolling sand and fine ground mineral ores.

Organon made a mental note that, in the event of space travel ever becoming possible for Chlorissians, he would give Tythonus a wide berth.

'You mean,' asked the Doctor, 'that without chlorophyll from Chloris your race will die out?' Then seizing the boss of the shield he waited for an answer.

'I wouldn't put it quite like that,' said Erato.

Romana stepped in. 'How would you put it?' she demanded. But fearing the Tythonian tendency towards prolixity, she added a rider to her question. 'In a word.'

Romana watched fascinated as the Doctor/Erato went purple with the effort to achieve brevity. 'The statement is substantially correct,' he agreed at length.

'Did you tell Adrasta all this?'

'I thought to appeal to her maternal feelings by pointing out the tragedy that would occur amongst the newborn of Tythonus should she refuse our generous offer. It was,' admitted Erato, 'a mistake. Apparently her species has no maternal feelings.'

I can believe that, thought the Doctor. On the other hand, why should Adrasta refuse the offer? It would have placed her in a very strong position in any negotiations.

Madam Karela and Adrasta had separated at a fork in the tunnel, Adrasta going to the right, Karela to the left. Karela hurried through the mine tunnels in the direction of Adrasta's Palace.

There, milling about at the foot of the steps that led up to the audience chamber, she found some of the guards who had fled, demoralised, from the Creature. They were standing around, arguing amongst themselves, at a loss to know what to do and in fear of their lives. The thought of facing the Lady Adrasta once again did not appeal to any of them. She would without doubt crucify them upside down in a vat of boiling ix juice.*

Madam Karela ordered the guards to follow her. They hesitated. It took her precisely ninety seconds, including a swift knife-thrust to the throat of the first and only vocal mutineer, before she restored order

*Ix juice is the sap of a hardwood tree indigenous to Chloris. Its sap closely resembles tar.

amongst the Lady Adrasta's troops; or to put it another way, before she persuaded the guards that they had more to fear from her than from any monster, no matter how large and no matter what colour.

This was always Madam Karela's way. Never waste time in idle discussion: act. She was a survivor; one had to be to make one's way in the savage society of Chloris. She was cruel, ruthless, murderous, and totally without scruple—which made her the ideal henchwoman for the Lady Adrasta. On other planets in other galaxies Karela would of course have retired long ago to spend her declining years spoiling her grandchildren and infuriating their parents. On Chloris she was still engaged in a bitter struggle for power. There were nights when, lying awake in her huge bedchamber where the candles burned all night and two Wolfweeds, chained to rings set in the wall, kept ceaseless watch in case of assassins, Adrasta herself wondered at the old woman's implacable spirit. One night, she thought, Karela will enter this chamber, knife in hand, determined to make herself sole ruler of Chloris. One night there will be reckoning. But now now.

In a side tunnel Karela and the guards came upon the Lady Adrasta driving her terrified huntsman and his flock of Wolfweeds before her. They were very reluctant to confront the Creature, but the Lady Adrasta was determined that they should, and the huntsman had to admit it was the lesser of two evils when Adrasta threatened to have him walled up with only his own Wolfweeds for company. In the past the weeds had revealed a disconcerting taste for human flesh, when starved of other game.

Having rallied their support, Karela and the Lady

Adrasta returned to the cavern to take the intruders by surprise.

At Adrasta's command Karela crept upon Organon, seized the unfortunate astrologer and put a knife to his throat. 'Tell your green friend to make no sudden moves, or else this old fool dies,' she warned the Doctor.

The Doctor smiled sadly at Organon, who was standing on tiptoe because of the knife that was pressing against the soft underside of his jaw. Organon looked pleadingly at the Doctor. 'I think she means it,' he said in a strangled voice, to avoid moving his chin.

'Yes, I think she does,' agreed the Doctor. 'Well, goodbye then, old friend. Thanks for all your help.'

Organon rose an extra millimetre or two and indignantly croaked, 'What do you mean—goodbye? You can't let her kill me.'

'I can't stop her, can I?' observed the Doctor, his voice full of sympthy. 'In any case Adrasta's determined to destroy Chloris. You and everyone else here,' he smiled at the guards, 'are as good as dead already. You're just going to die swiftly and cleanly and that much sooner than the rest of us. I'm really doing you a kindness, old friend.'

'I'd rather you didn't,' gasped Organon.

The guards shuffled uneasily. They lived in daily fear of their lives from the Lady Adrasta. But here was a new threat and one they didn't understand. 'Who's as good as dead already?' asked the huntsman.

'How is the Lady Adrasta going to destroy Chloris?' demanded one of the guards.

'It's obvious,' replied the Doctor. 'Just look at this planet. It's dying already: minimal cultivated land—and that's declining all the time; the jungle advancing everywhere, choking everything. Soon there'll be nothing but untamed forests and swamps. And why? Because you've got no metal to make tools to drain the swamps and cut back the jungle. And all because the Lady Adrasta controls the last remaining mine on Chloris.'

'Huntsman,' ordered Adrasta, 'set the Wolfweeds on this blasphemer!'

'Weeds!' shouted the Doctor angrily. 'That's the level of your civilisation! You've succeeded in cultivating weeds that are a danger to people: Wolfweeds, not plants that produce oil or vitamins or beefsteaks, but animated nettles that kill.

'Your friend the Ambassador,' went on the Doctor, patting the Creature, 'came here to bring you metals in exchange for some of your jungles. And what happened? The Lady Adrasta imprisoned him down here. Why? Because she feared that if anyone else controlled the mineral supply on Chloris she would lose the source of her political power. She's not merely a fool—she's a criminal fool!'

'Don't listen to him!' cried Adrasta. 'It's just the ravings of a demented space tramp.'

'Let him speak!' declared the huntsman.

'Yes, let him speak,' agreed several of the guards.

'No,' said the Doctor. 'Let the Tythonian Ambassador himself speak.' He gripped the shield once again. 'Keep it brief,' he whispered to Erato.

Erato told them how he had landed on Chloris fifteen years before. He had landed at night in order to cause the minimum of disturbance. Before dawn he had emerged from his craft and, with vocaliser (by which he meant the shield) in place, he had gone forth to make contact with the natives. Not surprisingly he had created something of a sensation. The first Chlorissians he had encountered had run away from him screaming. He found their reaction inexplicable. Nevertheless, it was clear that something about his personal appearance was offensive to the local inhabitants. But even now he could not conceive of what it could be. On Tythonus he was regarded as extremely handsome. It was one of the reasons why he had been selected as Ambassador.

'Get to the point,' whispered the Doctor.

Word of his presence had reached Adrasta. She and Karela and half a dozen heavily armed guards had come out to see what unexpected thing the jungle had brought forth. She didn't believe peasants' stories. Peasants always lied in her experience, either in hope of reward or else to evade taxes or punishment. But when they had come upon the Tythonian browsing on the vegetation, she realised at once it was not a native of Chloris.

In an attempt to establish friendly relations Erato had disgorged half a ton of pure copper at her feet. The sight of so much pure metal had overcome everyone's fear. Unfortunately it had excited Adrasta's natural cupidity.

Adrasta had sent her entourage away, except for one guard and Karela. And then she and Erato had communicated via the vocaliser, using the guard's larynx.

Once she had learned the purpose of his mission, Adrasta had sought for a way to turn it to her advantage. She agreed to negotiate, but insisted that he must come secretly to her Palace. She did not want to alarm her subjects any more than was necessary. There was, she declared, a secret way into the Palace from a nearby mine. Because the tunnels underground were narrow and rock-strewn she advised Erato to give her his vocaliser. She would take it straight to the Palace herself and it would be waiting for him on his arrival.

While uneasy about relinquishing his only means of communicating with the people of Chloris, Erato saw the sense of her plan. In any case he could not afford to antagonise the ruler of the planet, and he had no reason to suspect treachery.

Erato therefore agreed to travel to the Palace via the tunnels in the mine. With great difficulty he managed to slide his immense bulk down the mineshaft, whereupon Adrasta, Karela and the guard had piled rocks over the entrance to the shaft. Once in the mine he was trapped. There was no way out for him. The steps leading up to the Palace were barred by heavy doors and were in fact so steep and narrow that it was impossible for him to negotiate them.

Erato floundered around at the bottom of the mine wondering what to do. At first he presumed that Adrasta meant to keep him out of sight until she had prepared the population for his appearance. Then after a year or two it gradually dawned on him that she had trapped him in the mine hoping he would die.

Some time later a dozen heavily armed guards were lowered down the mineshaft. They had been sent to find out if he was still alive, and if so, to kill him. Unfortunately Erato had been so eager to communicate that he had rolled against them, forgetting for a moment that they weren't Tythonians. The guards had died of fear or suffocation. Over the years more Chlorissians were thrown down to him. Some were armed, some were not. Not that it mattered to the Tythonian—they all seemed to die no matter what he did.

At first he had worried that perhaps he had brought some terrible disease from the depths of space, some alien bacteria that caused Chlorissians to die the moment they saw him. But then after analysing a couple of the bodies he had rolled on he came to the conclusion that they were appallingly badly designed. They were a collection of impractical projections—arms, heads, legs—all of which broke so easily. It was not his fault, he decided, that his visitors failed to survive the encounter; it was a miracle they had survived thus far.

He had also made another discovery. The mine was worked out, or at least the primitive mining methods available to the Chlorissians were unable to extract any more metal ore. Then of course the significance of his discovery dawned on him. Adrasta needed him—not as a source of metal, but as an excuse to keep people out of her mine. With a monster in occupation it would take a brave man to go down into the Pit of his own volition. So no one need ever find out that the mine, the source of her political power, was finished. It was ironical, declared Erato, that until now Adrasta's political power had depended on him.

'They're lying!' said the Lady Adrasta. 'The Doctor and that Creature are lying. Or at least the Doctor is. You don't think for one second that a thing like that green blob can actually talk, do you?'

'It's easy enough to find out,' replied the Doctor. 'Try it yourself. Try holding on to the vocaliser and see what happens. Perhaps we can learn the truth from your own lips.'

Adrasta shrank away from the Doctor. She looked desperately round for Karela. Where was she?

‘Come on,’ said the Doctor. ‘Don’t you want the truth to be known?’

‘You don’t expect intelligent men like my guards to be taken in by these childish tricks,’ sneered Adrasta. ‘Huntsman, kill the Doctor.’

But the huntsman didn’t move.

‘Guards!’

They too showed no sign of obeying her orders.

Damn them. Where was Karela?

‘Speak with the Creature,’ ordered the huntsman. Adrasta glared at him. ‘I will devise a way of killing you,’ she declared, ‘so painfully and so slowly that the torments of hell will seem a pleasure by comparison.’

The huntsman cracked his whip. Obediently the Wolfweeds moved towards her. She backed away. Again the huntsman urged on the Wolfweeds. Again Adrasta moved away. But she was being driven towards Erato.

The Doctor suddenly stepped forward and seized her by the wrist. He forced her hand on the handle of the vocaliser.

Adrasta screamed and tried to tear her hand away. But she could not. From her lips came her own voice condemning her.

‘It is as I said,’ declared Adrasta/Erato. ‘This evil woman condemned me, the Tythonian Ambassador, to fifteen years in this foul-smelling pit. For fifteen years I have not felt the gentle sulphuric acid rain of Tythonus on my skin. For fifteen years I have been deprived of the songs and poetry of my native planet, of communication with civilised creatures. I have fifteen years of pain and misery and anguish to avenge.’

Suddenly, with a swiftness that surprised everyone,

the enormous green mass moved. Erato rolled over the Lady Adrasta and the Wolfweeds like an avalanche. After a few moments he rolled back. The Wolfweeds were gone. The Lady Adrasta lay dead, her eyes wide open in a state of pure horror.

The Doctor seized the vocaliser. 'Thank you,' said the Doctor/Erato. 'The Wolfweeds were delicious.'

10

Complications

Tucking into his first proper meal for weeks, Organon waxed indignant with Romana. 'He was going to let me die,' he complained. 'My friend, the man I saved from that green thing, was going to let me die.

'I tell you,' he went on, waving the leg of a cold roast fondel* in her direction, 'there's no gratitude in the world.'

Romana looked up from picking the last Wolfweed filaments off K9. 'Of course the Doctor wouldn't have let you die,' she declared. 'It was all a ploy to get Adrasta off balance.'

'Well, it got me off balance, I can tell you. He might have more consideration for my age,' he added.

'It worked, didn't it? You're out of the Pit, aren't you? You're alive and well and eating your fourth fondel leg, unless I'm mistaken. And this planet now has a future—if Erato is to be believed.'

'I'm not sure that he is,' said the Doctor, entering the audience chamber.

Organon choked on a piece of fondel. The Doctor patted him on the back.

'What do you mean about Erato?' demanded Romana.

* A fondel is a kind of wild turkey peculiar to Chloris.

'Well, in spite of what he says, I don't believe that our large green friend was made an Ambassador just because of his looks.' The Doctor removed the last roast fondel leg from Organon's plate, dipped it in the uxal sauce*, and took a bite. 'Delicious,' he announced.

'You were telling us about Erato,' Romana reminded him.

'Well, he is a very shrewd, very experienced planetary negotiator. Unless I miss my guess, he has several nasty suprises up his sleeve—or tucked in the folds of his extraordinary green cerebellum. This really is very good,' he went on, dipping the leg into the uxal sauce once again.

'I don't like suprises,' observed Organon gloomily. 'After a lifetime in the astrology business, I can assure you that in my experience suprises have a habit of being singularly unpleasant.'

'If that's the case,' demanded Romana, 'why are you getting Erato out of the Pit? I mean he might go off in his spacecraft and return with a load of angry Tythonians. How did he arrive here?' she asked.

'In an egg.'

'The broken shell we found.'

The Doctor nodded. 'When it's in one piece, it's actually a blindingly simple space vehicle, complete with photon drive.'

'We didn't see any photon drive.'

'I did,' said the Doctor. 'He took some pieces of shell with him down the Pit. I found them there. One of the pieces is a photon drive.'

Romana looked worried. 'When we found that shell,

*Uxal sauce is a kind of chutney made from uxal berries.

it was transmitting some kind of message. What?'

'Obviously a distress signal.'

'If it was transmitting a distress signal for fifteen years,' pointed out Organon, 'surely the things on Tythonus would have done something about it by now.'

'Maybe they have,' replied the Doctor.

'What?'

'I don't know. That rather depends on the Tythonians.' The Doctor scooped up a gobbet of uxal sauce on his finger and thoughtfully sucked it off. 'One thing I do know,' he said at last, 'is that our green friend won't be leaving Chloris in a hurry.'

'What's to stop him?'

'Because,' replied the Doctor, removing a curiously shaped piece of eggshell from his pocket, 'I took the precaution of borrowing part of his photon drive.'

At considerable risk to life and limb, Edu clung to the window embrasure, peering into the audience chamber. Ainu and Torvin held his legs.

'What can you see?' whispered Torvin.

'That Doctor chap waving something about,' replied Edu in a hoarse whisper.

'Is it metal?'

'Don't know.'

Edu suddenly ducked down.

'What is it?'

'One of the guards has just come in.'

The guard in fact had brought news for the Doctor. The Tythonian was now out of the Pit at last and on his way to the Palace.

Tollund, the late Lady Adrasta's senior engineer, had been busy. At the Doctor's directions and working intensively for the past few hours, he had widened the mouth of the pitshaft and had built a wooden ramp from the base of the shaft to the surface—a ramp strong enough and wide enough to take Erato. With the aid of four great windlasses and several hundred men Erato had managed to mount the ramp and squeeze himself through the opening.

'Are you coming?' Romana asked Organon.

The old man shuddered and shook his head. 'No, thank you,' he said firmly. 'I saw enough of that monster down the Pit to last me several lifetimes. I have no desire to renew the acquaintance. Besides I haven't finished eating yet.'

The Doctor placed the piece of shell on the table. 'Guard that with your life,' he said.

'You may rely on me,' replied the astrologer, picking up a large piece of pie.

'They've gone,' said Edu, peering through the window again, 'all except for that old astrologer.'

'What's he doing?' asked Torvin.

'Eating.'

It had taken all Torvin's inconsiderable powers of persuasion to get Ainu and Edu to return to the Palace with him. The rest of the band had fled. One close encounter with the Tythonian had been enough to encourage them to put the maximum distance between themselves and the mine. Ainu and Edu remained loyal (if that was the word) thanks to a unique combination of greed and stupidity; Ainu was greedy, Edu stupid.

'Come on down,' hissed Torvin.

The little pockmarked bandit lowered himself from the window and dropped to the floor.

'This,' declared Torvin with a confidence he did not possess, 'is where we make our fortunes.'

An extraordinary sight met the Doctor and Romana when they descended to the courtyard of the Palace. Erato was in the act of squeezing the first few feet of himself through the main gate. The rest of him stretched back into the jungle. They could see tendrils emerging from his body which were delicately stripping the greenery from the surrounding trees and bushes.

If something as shapeless as the Tythonian could be said to have an expression, then Erato was positively beaming. His veins (if they were veins) were pulsing brightly and his skin glowed with well-being.

The Doctor nodded to Romana who stepped forward and took hold of the handle of the volcaliser. 'I think it's time you answered a few questions, my friend,' the Doctor said.

'With pleasure,' replied Romana/Erato. 'But first you really must compliment our hosts. Their leaves are delicious.'

'Let's talk about your distress signal first, the one in the shell at the Place of Death. Unless I'm mistaken, it's been transmitting direct to Tythonus for the past fifteen years. Am I right?'

'Correct.'

'Shouldn't you switch it off now?'

'It will have switched itself off, the moment I came out of the Pit. It is telepathically connected to one of my neurological centres.'

'Then we've nothing to worry about?'

Erato did not reply.

'Have we?' demanded the Doctor.

'Well, I'd rather not talk about it,' said the Tythonian with obvious embarrassment. 'I don't wish to cause distress and despondency. Besides I'm afraid it's far too late to do anything about it now.'

'Too late to do anything about what?'

'Believe me, I would prevent it if I could,' went on Erato.

'What would you prevent if you could?'

'I mean, it's hardly something one is going to look back on over the next twenty thousand years or so with pride.'

'What?'

'The total destruction of this solar system.'

The Doctor stared at the Creature in astonishment, hardly able to believe his ears. Perhaps being imprisoned in the mine for fifteen years had affected the Tythonian. It was inconceivable that a few green blobs, however huge, could destroy a whole solar system.

'Are you quite sure?' he asked.

'Absolutely.'

'The forces required to destroy a solar system—even quite a small one—are, well, astronomic.'

'Precisely,' agreed Erato. 'Which is why we use a neutron star.'

'A neutron star?'

'A collapsed star composed of supercompressed degenerate matter,' explained Erato helpfully.

'I know what a neutron star is,' snapped the Doctor. 'I just don't know what you propose to do with it.'

'Bounce it off one of Chloris's suns,' replied Erato. 'It's really very simple.'

Erato went on to explain that the Tythonians were a peace-loving race. They had not fought a war for over a million years. They didn't need to, because they had developed the supreme doomsday weapon. Their power of retaliation was so enormous no adversary was prepared to risk total annihiliation.

About two million years ago they had discovered how to affect the orbits of neutron stars, of which there were a great number in the galaxy. They could in fact direct the star into the path of a particular solar system. Great accuracy was not required. All the neutron star had to do was to brush the surface of a sun and ...

'Bang,' said Erato simply. 'There's an explosion.'

'That,' replied the Doctor, 'has to be the understatement of the millenium. What you're suggesting would create a fireball a tenth of a light year across.'

'Yes.'

'Well, stop it,' demanded the Doctor. 'Abort the missile. Transmit a new message from the shell, telling your people on Tythonus that you are alive and well and having a marvellous time. And get them to stop the star.'

Romana/Erato sighed regretfully. 'I'm very much afraid that's impossible, Doctor,' he said. 'That's the trouble with neutron stars—once you've started them on their way you can't stop them. I did warn the Lady Adrasta,' he went on, 'that if I, as Tythonian Ambassador, was in any way harmed, then she would face retaliation on a scale she could not conceive. Unfortunately she was a very stupid woman.'

The Doctor thought hard for a moment. There had to be some way of preventing the tragedy.

'There's one solution,' he said at last. 'We'll just have to transfer the population of Chloris to another planet in another solar system. It's going to take time. But it's not impossible. How long have we got before the neutron star strikes?' he asked.

'Approximately twenty-four hours.'

In the cold and empty reaches of space the neutron star sped on its way. There were no astronomers on any of the neighbouring planetary systems to observe its passage. If there had been they would have written learned papers on the subject, full of theories explaining such a unique event.

Long ago the star had consumed all its own nuclear fuel. Long ago its own source of energy had died. Now gravitational forces of unimaginable magnitude compressed it—until it was no more than ten kilometres in diameter: about half the size of London. Now it was no more than a thin outer shell containing nothing but neutrons.

Dead but deadly, it came ever closer to the smallest of Chloris's suns. Already there were signs of perturbation on the surface of the suns.

'I would love to stay,' said Erato, backing away from the Doctor and trying to manoeuvre his bulk back through the Palace gates. 'But I really must go now. Do forgive me. I am a sentimentalist at heart and have no wish to be a witness to the inevitable distressing scenes that are bound to occur when the star strikes one of Chloris's suns.'

Romana and the Doctor followed him, the former still keeping a tight hold on the vocaliser. Their presence was obviously beginning to irritate the Tythonian, who wished to be on his way.

Erato stopped in his tracks. 'Look. There really is no point in you following me,' he said. 'I would strongly advise you to make your own escape as soon as you can from this, alas, doomed planet. I understand that you have a time and space vehicle of your own. Use it now.'

'How will you escape?' asked the Doctor.

'Don't worry about me,' continued Erato, beginning to back away again. 'I'll just make myself another spacecraft.'

'But that will take ages.'

'Three Tythonian ninods. Or one hour seven seconds in your time.'

Build a space ship in a hour? Impossible, thought the Doctor. On the other hand, I suppose if you can shunt neutron stars around the Universe like so many cattle trucks, anything is possible. There again, of course, a Tythonian spacecraft isn't a particularly complex machine. If the broken shell at the Place of Death was anything to go by, it was really no more than a huge egg equipped with photon drive. Though when you looked at Erato spread over the surrounding countryside, the sheer immensity of the operation boggled the mind.

Then the Doctor remembered the strange metallic threads which the Tythonian had secreted, like a spider, in order to construct the shell-like barrier in the mine. That must be how he made his spaceship.

'You mean you just sort of knit yourself a spaceship?' the Doctor asked.

Erato was offended at this implied slighting of his talents. 'It's not quite as simple as that,' he snapped. 'There's a knack to it, you know. Not every Tythonian succeeds in mastering the art. Which is why only a few of my race are space travellers.'

Thank heavens for that, thought Romana. Not that she personally had anything against Erato—except for the fact that he had nearly frightened her out of her wits on several occasions. But she was relieved to learn that they wouldn't be meeting huge green blobs on every planet where they made landfall.

'Don't be so touchy,' said the Doctor. 'I'm impressed. Can you knit anything?'

'Like what?'

'Like several kilometres of aluminium foil.'

'Why would I wish to do that?' demanded the Tythonian.

An abstracted expression came over the Doctor's face. He stared blankly at a small lizard-like creature that was trying to climb the Palace wall and failing. An idea was beginning to form in his brain—an idea so extraordinary, so lunatic, it just might work.

'Would you be prepared to save this planet from your doomsday weapon?' he asked. 'It might be just a bit risky, of course,' he went on, aware that that hardly described the extreme danger inherent in his plan. 'But it could prevent the destruction of Chloris.'

Erato, however, had little reason to feel friendly towards his ex-captors.

'Let me remind you, Doctor,' he said. 'I came to this benighted planet as an accredited Ambassador, with an offer to help its unfortunate inhabitants. They imprisoned me for fifteen years in a disgusting hole in the ground and would have starved me to death, if that had been possible.'

'I know, I know,' replied the Doctor soothingly. 'Believe me, you have my sympathy. But after all, the Chlorissians were not responsible for the actions of that madwoman, the Lady Adrasta.'

'I am not so sure of that,' replied the Tythonian. 'I didn't notice any of them rushing to free me. In any case, I am disinclined to commit suicide on their behalf. And that is precisely what it would be if I stayed here.'

'I thought the Tythonians were a peace-loving race.'

'We are.'

'Then I would have thought you, as Tythonian Ambassador, would want to make a positive demonstration of Tythonian good will.'

Erato considered the matter for a moment. Unfortunately he had to admit that the Doctor's argument was irresistible. He regretted the necessity of destroying a planet so rich in valuable chlorophyll—a planet which held the promise of feeding generations of young Tythonians. And he loathed the prospect of causing such an appalling loss of life.

'Oh, very well,' he said pettishly. 'I will help.'

The Doctor sighed with relief. For without the Tythonian's help his plan had no chance of success.

'What do you want me to do?'

'Knit a thin aluminium shell round the neutron star. That should minimise its gravitational pull, so we can then yank it out of its present orbit.'

'And how do we do the "yanking"?'

'We use the TARDIS,' explained the Doctor, 'as a tractor beam. We can exert short bursts of enormous gravitational pressure on the star, which should be enough to slow it up, so that you can wrap it in an aluminium shell.'

Romana released the handle of the vocaliser. 'That's crazy, Doctor,' she objected.

'You stay out of this,' he replied.

Romana took hold of the vocaliser once again.

'I agree with Romana,' said Erato. 'She is quite correct. It is a recipe for mutual destruction.'

The Doctor did not reply.

'On the other hand,' went on the Tythonian after a moment, 'it just—just—might work.'

'Then you'll help?'

'Very well.'

'I knew you would.'

Erato was curious. 'What would you have done if I had decided to abandon you? I could have built my spaceship and returned home.'

'You might have found that a bit tricky. You see, I took the precaution of removing a vital part of your photon drive,' confessed the Doctor. 'There's no way you could have left this planet.'

Unfortunately, as the Doctor and Romana were to discover, that was all too true. When they returned to the audience chamber, they found Organon unconscious, but still clutching the remains of a half-eaten pie. But the piece of shell with the photon drive had vanished.

In the corner of the Palace courtyard, creepers and lianas grew outwards to form a kind of shelter sometimes used by guards who wished to take cover from the rain. It was from there that Madam Karela had watched the meeting between the Doctor and the Creature. She had not been able to overhear much of their conversation. But she had heard enough for her purposes. At last, after all her years of loyal service to the Lady Adrasta, after all her years of patience and plotting, she saw a way of assuming supreme power on Chloris. The day of Karela had arrived. She slipped silently away.

It wasn't difficult for her to follow the bandits in their progress through the jungle. Success had made them careless. She stalked them like an elderly but still lethal panther, her black clothes making her almost invisible in the twilight of the overshadowing trees. She was never far behind the three men, yet never for a moment did they realise she was there.

Torvin, Ainu and Edu stopped constantly to argue. Edu had wanted to keep the piece of shell the old astrologer had been guarding. He had taken a fancy to it. But Torvin was insistent: no useless baggage; They had enough to carry as it was.

'We found Adrasta's metal vault, didn't we?' demanded Torvin. 'We're loaded up with the real thing, aren't we? Copper. Iron. Tin. What do we want with a broken piece of shell?'

'Maybe it's valuable,' objected Edu.

'Metal! That's what's important!' shouted Torvin, belabouring the little pockmarked man with the flat of a bronze sword. 'Metal, you moron!'

'You always pick on me,' complained Edu.

'Pick on you? Be careful I don't pick your bones one day, you half-pint apology for a nonentity.'

Sulkily Edu threw away the piece of shell.

The bandits reached their cave and unloaded their booty. They emptied their sacks out on the floor. They had only spent a few hurried moment in Adrasta's vault, but it was amazing how much they had managed to take: ingots of copper; tin beaten into thin leaf shapes; rods of iron; bronze objects decorated in the linear style favoured 150 years ago; swords, axes, votive vessels. Torvin positively drooled over the haul. 'And you wanted to bother about a piece of rotten old shell!' he scoffed to Edu.

They were so occupied with their booty, none of them noticed Karela enter the cave. She paused, summing up the situation. What a pathetic bunch of cut-throats! That she should be reduced to seeking the help of scum like this! Unfortunately she needed them—but not their leader, she thought.

'Look at it,' rhapsodised Torvin, stroking an elegant bronze drinking mug. 'Undamaged. No rust anywhere. Just like new.'

He gave a gasp as Karela, with the deftness of long practice, inserted her knife blade just below his rib cage on the left-hand side and drove the point upwards. Torvin looked down in astonishment to see the point of the knife emerge from his chest. 'Tempered steel?' he murmured in surprise, and died.

With a swift movement, using her knee in the small of his back to provide leverage, Karela withdrew the knife as he fell. She turned to face the other two.

'He's dead,' said Edu. 'You killed him.'

Ainu wasted no time in idle conversation. He drew his own knife.

'Kill me and you condemn yourself to poverty,' she warned. She indicated the pile of metal on the floor. 'You think this is wealth? This is nothing compared with what we can have, you and I. We could fill this cave a hundred times over with pure metal.'

Ainu moved a step towards her, then paused as her words sank in. 'Metal?'

Karela smiled inwardly. Greed she understood. You could always handle greed. Stupidity was apt to be dangerous, though.

'She killed Torvin,' said Edu plaintively.

'Anybody might be excused for doing that,' observed

Karela. 'He seemed a thoroughly unpleasant man. And I never even knew him.'

'He was unpleasant,' agreed Edu. 'But he was our leader.'

'What's all this about caves full of metal?' demanded Ainu, circling away a little to his left, so that Karela was between the two of them. She is quick with that knife, he thought. But the two of us should be able to tackle her.

Karela pointed to the pile of copper ingots. 'You know where that copper came from? From the Creature. I was there when he laid half a ton of pure copper at the Lady Adrasta's feet. I helped weigh it. I know. Half a ton of copper—think of it.'

Ainu and Edu thought of it. It was a pleasant thought.

'It came from the Creature?' asked Edu.

Karela nodded. 'And he will produce more: as much as we want.'

'Why should he?' demanded Ainu suspiciously.

'Because he needs that piece of shell you stole.'

The two bandits stared at each other in horror. 'Torvin made me throw it away,' said Edu. 'I told him ...'

'Yes, but I found it. I have it hidden. What I need,' went on Karela, 'is two men I can trust. I have to deal with Romana and the Doctor. I cannot do it alone. You will help me kill them, then together we can seize power here on Chloris and force the Creature to give us as much metal as we want.'

'There's only one problem with that scenario,' said the Doctor from the cave mouth. 'In a very few hours all that will be left of this planet is several trillion tons of deep-fried rubble. Still fancy going into the metal business?'

With the help of K9, the Doctor had been able to follow the tracks of the bandits and Madam Karela through the jungle. He had stood outside the cave long enough to be able to guess at the evil woman's plans.

'Deep-fried rubble?' said Edu uneasily. 'What does he mean—deep-fried rubble?'

'He's only trying to frighten you,' declared Madam Karela. 'Nothing's going to happen. Don't listen to him. Kill him.'

K9 pushed his way into the cave and stood beside the Doctor.

The bandits stared at the robot unhappily, remembering how it had once dealt with the late Torvin. At last Ainu re-sheathed his knife and shook his head. 'I've met that metal animal before,' he said.

Karela turned angrily on the bandits. 'Cowards!' she snarled. 'Do I have to do all the killing myself?'

'Before you do anything you'll regret later,' said the Doctor, 'tell me where you've hidden that piece of shell. It's rather important.'

Knife in hand, her eyes blazing, Karela took a step towards the Doctor.

'We could find that piece of shell ourselves,' went on the Doctor. 'But it would take time. And time is the one thing we haven't got.'

Karela moved closer. K9's sensors twitched uneasily. He was ready to fire the instant she attempted to strike at the Doctor. But the Doctor wanted to avoid the necessity of stunning her. She might be unconscious for a half an hour. There just wasn't time. Every second the neutron star was growing nearer to Chloris's suns.

'You still think that piece of shell is you key to power on Chloris?' he asked. 'You still think you can use it to force the Creature to give you all the metal you want? Well, go ahead. You're welcome to anything produced by our friend Erato.'

Karela paused, frowning.

'You see,' said the Doctor, 'the trouble is, the metal isn't atomically stable.'

'You're lying,' insisted Karela. 'Those ingots are copper. Adrasta and I tested them ourselves.'

'Of course they're copper. But it's unusable. Show her, K9.'

K9 turned his ray onto the booty heaped on the cave floor. There was a curious humming noise which grew steadily in intensity. The copper ingots lost their brightness, became dull. They turned black ... then began to disintegrate ... gradually crumbling to dust. When K9 switched off his ray, the only remains of the copper was a pile of greyish dust.

Madam Karela aged visibily as she watched the process of destruction. She saw her last chance of taking supreme political power on Chloris fading away in front of her, like morning mist in the sun.

'The dream's over,' said the Doctor gently. 'Tell me where that piece of shell is.'

11

Wrapping Up

'How did you know the copper would disintegrate?' asked Romana, while they watched Erato making his space ship. It was an unforgettable sight. Glittering metallic threads emerged from his body and began to weave a silvery web around him.

'The Tythonians are a cautious, canny race,' explained the Doctor. 'Maybe it's why they've survived so long. They always seem to build some kind of back-up system into everything they construct. The shell, for example, went on transmitting even while Erato was in the Pit. The neutron star was automatically triggered on its way by the shell.'

By now Erato was completely covered by a think cocoon of gleaming threads. More threads spilled out of the cocoon, criss-crossing each other, building up the structure.

'In any case,' went on the Doctor, 'I always wondered about that copper Erato gave Adrasta. I thought there had to be a catch in it somewhere. There had to be some way he could take back his gift if Adrasta reneged on him. The molecular structure of the metal was rearranged slightly, so that it reacted to certain resonances. All K9 had to do was to find the resonating factor, and Bob's your Uncle—half a hundred weight of dust.'

'Talking of K9,' said Romana, 'shouldn't we be fixing up that communication bank for him? Erato will soon be ready to take off.'

'Erato, can you hear me?' asked the Doctor. 'Testing. Testing.'

'I can hear you,' replied K9.

They were back in the TARDIS. The robot was plugged into a freestanding communications console, his vocal circuits locked into Erato's vocaliser. The Tythonian was therefore able to speak through K9.

'Preparing for take off,' said Erato.

On the large videoscreen in the TARDIS Romana watched the great silver egg rise slowly and silently into the air.

'It reminds me of something they used to have on Earth,' remarked the Doctor. 'They called them zeppelins. Trouble was the old Count never could get the design right.'

Suddenly the silver egg changed attitude. Its nose lifted until it pointed skywards. There was a faint blur of light around the vessel, and then it hurled itself in the direction of Chloris's suns.

The Doctor stood at the control console, making minute adjustments, checking the setting of all the dials. 'This has got to be absolutely precise,' he remarked. 'There's no room for error.'

'That'll be a change,' said Romana.

'Any sign of that neutron star yet?' he asked.

She checked the small display screen. 'There's a blip on Band Six,' she replied. 'I'll increase the resolution.' She adjusted the controls then, when the image was steady, punched the picture up on the videoscreen.

They were now looking deep into space. And there,

thousands of kilometres away, they saw, faintly at first but growing larger all the time, the Tythonians' doomsday weapon—the neutron star.

'There it is,' she said.

'Well, no point in hanging around here,' observed the Doctor.

He threw the switch. The central column on the control console of the TARDIS began to rise and fall. Lights flashed. They heard the familiar sound of the TARDIS de-materialising. And a blue police box vanished from the surface of Chloris.

As Erato's craft cautiously approached the neutron star, so the Tardis re-materialised close by.

'Oops,' said the Doctor. 'Bit too close. Sorry.'

'Watch what you're doing,' snapped K9. 'I have no desire to get caught in your time eddy.'

'I never said this was going to be easy,' replied the Doctor.

Erato did not reply. He was occupied taking readings of the star through his sensors. 'Doctor,' he said at last, 'the star is gathering momentum. Very shortly it's going to be subject to an irresistible gravitational pull from Chloris's suns. Are you sure you can hold it while I surround the thing with an aluminium shell?'

The Doctor checked the calculations he had hastily scribbled on the back of an old laundry list. 'Frankly, no,' he said. 'To be absolutely honest, old thing, I haven't used the gravity tractor beam since ...' He couldn't remember the last time. 'Well, about ten years ago. I always meant to check the blessed thing, but I never actually got round to it.'

'Now you tell me,' replied Erato glumly.

'There's only one way to find out.'

The Doctor activated the tractor beam.

The TARDIS shuddered. Its exterior became incandescent. The whole machine screamed and groaned. The needles on a dozen dials shot over into the area marked 'Danger'. Red warning lights flashed on.

Romana watched on the videoscreen as Erato began to move closer to the star. She saw the first silvery threads emerge from the egg and drift across the intervening space. Suddenly the picture distorted. Images multiplied. Half a dozen Eratos approached half a dozen stars. The control room of the TARDIS took on a nightmarish appearance. Walls seemed to concertina in and out. The floor rippled. There were no fewer than three consoles. Two Doctors leapt across to them and threw the switches. With that everything returned to normal.

'We can't hold that star for more than five seconds,' said Romana. 'The effect of the tractor beam is to distort our spatial dimension.'

'Doctor,' said K9, 'you must hold the star. I'm being dragged towards it.'

The Doctor and Romana glanced up at the videoscreen. They saw Erato's craft was plunging out of control towards the star.

'Nothing to worry about,' said the Doctor, with a cheerfulness he didn't feel. He crossed his fingers, kicked the console, and threw the gravity traction beam switch once again.

This time, except for occasional distortions, the beam held.

'All right, Erato,' he said. 'Get weaving.'

Erato began to circle the star, gradually wrapping it in a web of silvery threads, cocooning it in a shell of aluminium.

Worriedly Romana checked on the dials. The needles were beginning to creep up towards the 'Danger' area again. 'We're placing a terrible strain on the TARDIS,' she said. 'How much longer, Erato?'

'You can turn off your gravity beam in five of your seconds,' replied K9. 'Counting now ... Five ... four ... three ... two ... One ...'

Erato never got any further because just at that point part of the control console of the TARDIS blew up, hurling the Doctor and Romana against the wall.

'What happened? cried Romana.

The Doctor fought his way back to the console. 'The control circuit's gone! We can't switch off the beam. We're pulling the star in towards us.'

The star, a great aluminium-covered ball, filled the videoscreen.

Pulled by the gravity traction beam it was rushing to collide with the TARDIS.

'Doctor,' cried Romana, 'we've got to dematerialise.'

With the star almost upon them the Doctor managed to press the dematerialisation button.

The star passed harmlessly through the space previously occupied by the TARDIS.

When they rematerialised, they saw the star on the videoscreen. It was swinging away on a new orbit—an orbit that would take it far from the suns of Chloris.

'I still say it was impossible,' said K9/Erato.

Romana agreed. 'I worked out that our chances of success were 74,384,338 to 11 against.'

'74,384,338 just happens to be my lucky number,' said the Doctor.

CHILDREN'S BOOKS

	ISBN	Author / Title	Price
	0426105672	SPIKE MILLIGAN **Badjelly the Witch (illus)**	£1.25
	0426109546	SPIKE MILLIGAN **Dip the Puppy (illus)**	60p
	0426117891	JOYCE NICHOLSON **Freedom for Priscilla**	70p
	0426119223	MARY RODGERS **A Billion for Boris**	60p
Δ	0426200152	BARBARA EUPHAN TODD **Detective Worzel Gummidge (illus)**	60p
Δ	04626201272	**Earthy Mangold and Worzel Gummidge**	95p
Δ	04626201280	**Worzel Gummidge and the Circus**	75p

'DOCTOR WHO'

	ISBN	Author / Title	Price
Δ	0426114558	TERRANCE DICKS **Doctor Who and the Abominable Snowman**	70p
Δ	0426200373	**Doctor Who and the Android Invasion**	90p
Δ	0426201086	**Doctor Who and The Androids of Tara**	75p
Δ	0426201043	**Doctor Who and The Armageddon Factor**	85p
Δ	0426112954	TERRANCE DICKS **Doctor Who and The Auton Invasion**	75p

DOCTOR WHO

	ISBN	Title	Price
Δ	0426116747	Doctor Who and The Brain of Morbius	75p
Δ	0426110250	Doctor Who and The Carnival of Monsters	85p
Δ	042611471X	MALCOLM HULKE Doctor Who and The Cave-Monsters	75p
Δ	0426117034	TERRANCE DICKS Doctor Who and The Claws of Axos	75p
Δ	042620123X	DAVID FISHER Doctor Who and the Creature from the Pit	90p
Δ	0426113160	DAVID WHITAKER Doctor Who and The Crusaders	75p
	0426114639	GERRY DAVIS Doctor Who and The Cybermen	85p
Δ	0426113322	TERRANCE DICKS Doctor Who and The Daemons	75p
Δ	042611244X	Doctor Who and The Dalek Invasion of Earth	85p
Δ	0426103807	Doctor Who and the Day of the Daleks	85p
Δ	0426119657	TERRANCE DICKS Doctor Who and the Deadly Assassin	85p
Δ	042620042X	Doctor Who–Death to the Daleks	75p
Δ	0426200969	Doctor Who and the Destiny of the Daleks	75p
Δ	0426108744	MALCOLM HULKE Doctor Who and the Dinosaur Invasion	75p

'DOCTOR WHO'

	ISBN	Author / Title	Price
Δ	0426103726	Doctor Who and the Doomsday Weapon	85p
Δ	0426200063	TERRANCE DICKS Doctor Who and the Face of Evil	85p
Δ	0426112601	Doctor Who and the Genesis of The Daleks	75p
Δ	0426112792	Doctor Who and the Giant Robot	85p
Δ	0426115430	MALCOLM HULKE Doctor Who and the Green Death	75p
Δ	0426200330	TERRANCE DICKS Doctor Who and the Hand of Fear	75p
Δ	0426201310	Doctor Who and the Horns of Nimon	85p
Δ	0426108663	BRIAN HAYLES Doctor Who and the Ice Warriors	85p
Δ	0426200772	TERRANCE DICKS Doctor Who and the Image of The Fendahl	75p
Δ	0426200772	Doctor Who and the Image of The Fendahl	75p
Δ	0426200934	Doctor Who and the Invasion of Time	75p
Δ	0426200543	Doctor Who and the Invisible Enemy	75p
Δ	0426201256	PHILIP HINCHCLIFFE Doctor Who and the Keys of Marinus	85p
Δ	0426110412	TERRANCE DICKS Doctor Who and the Loch Ness Monster	85p

DOCTOR WHO

		PHILIP HINCHCLIFFE	
Δ	0426118936	**Doctor Who and the Masque of Mandragora**	**85p**
		TERRANCE DICKS	
	0426201329	**Doctor Who and the Monster of Peladon**	**85p**
Δ	0426201302	**Doctor Who and the Nightmare of Eden**	**85p**
Δ	0426112520	**Doctor Who and the Planet of the Daleks**	**75p**
Δ	0426106555	**Dr Who and the Planet of the Spiders**	**85p**
Δ	0426201019	**Doctor Who and the Power of Kroll**	**85p**
Δ	0426200616	**Doctor Who and the Robots of Death**	**90p**
		MALCOLM HULKE	
Δ	042611308X	**Doctor Who and the Sea Devils**	**90p**
		PHILIP HINCHCLIFFE	
Δ	0426116585	**Doctor Who and the Seeds of Doom**	**85p**
		IAN MARTER	
Δ	0426200497	**Doctor Who and the Sontaren Experiment**	**60p**
		MALCOLM HULKE	
Δ	0426110331	**Doctor Who and the Space War**	**85p**
		TERRANCE DICKS	
Δ	0426200993	**Doctor Who and the Stones of Blood**	**75p**
		TERRANCE DICKS	
Δ	0426119738	**Doctor Who and the Talons of Weng Chiang**	**75p**
		GERRY DAVIS	
Δ	0426110684	**Doctor Who and the Tenth Planet**	**85p**

DOCTOR WHO

	ISBN	Title	Price
Δ	0426115007	TERRANCE DICKS **Doctor Who and the Terror of the Autons**	75p
Δ	0426115783	**Doctor Who and the Three Doctors**	85p
Δ	0426200233	**Doctor Who and the Time Warrior**	75p
Δ	0426200683	TERRANCE DICKS **Doctor Who and the Underworld**	75p
Δ	0426200829	MALCOLM HULKE **Doctor Who and the War Games**	85p
Δ	0426110846	TERRANCE DICKS **Doctor Who and the Web of Fear**	75p
	0426200675	TERRANCE DICKS **The Adventures of K9 and other Mechanical Creatures (illus)**	75p
	0426200950	**Terry Nation's Dalek Special (illus)**	95p
	0426200012	**The Second Doctor Who Monster Book (Colour illus)**	70p
	0426118421	**Doctor Who Dinosaur Book (illus)**	75p

DOCTOR WHO

	ISBN	Title	Price
	0426200020	Doctor Who Discovers Prehistoric Animals (NF) (illus)	75p
	0426200039	Doctor Who Discovers Space Travel (NF) (illus)	75p
	0426200047	Doctor Who Discovers Strange and Mysterious Creatures (NF) (illus)	75p
	042620008X	Doctor Who Discovers the Story of Early Man (NF) (illus)	75p
	0426200136	Doctor Who Discovers the Conquerors (NF) (illus)	75p
Δ	0426200632	Junior Doctor Who: Brain of Moribus	90p
	0426116151	TERRANCE DICKS AND MALCOLM HULKE The Making of Doctor Who	95p